Amber Guardians Workbook

Contents

Amber Guardians Workbook introduction

Amber Guardians Workbook is loosely linked to the Amber Guardians reading series. This workbook focuses on helping students learn to read, spell and comprehend using their knowledge and understanding of English morphemes. Each chapter has cloze activities based on the text in the reading series. Other activities are independent of the reading series. The numbered chapters in this workbook correlate to the books in the reading series but do not have to be used strictly in tandem.

Beyond phonics

In previous series and workbooks, the importance of linking sound to spellings when learning to read and spell has been emphasized. The student has been taught to read a word by decoding (reading) graphemes on the page and to spell by encoding (spelling) graphemes that represent the sounds in a word. He/she has also been taught to split words into syllables when reading and spelling words with more than one syllable. The next stage is to help the student develop his/her understanding of how the English language works at the morphemic level. Morphemes are units of meaning in a word. Recent research has shown that teaching students to identify morphemes and their meanings will help them improve their literacy in general. For example, it is useful for the student to understand the purpose of the suffix 'ed' at the end of a word, and how to spell words when the suffix 'ed' is added to them.

This workbook introduces a range of suffixes, prefixes and root words which will teach students to identify the meaning of parts of the word and to make links and connections to new words they encounter. This understanding will help them extend their vocabulary and, as a result, their comprehension. It will also help them to improve their spelling.

Splitting words into syllables and morphemes

Splitting words into syllables (chunks of sounds within a word) is essential when the reader encounters a new word. This is a different approach to breaking words up into morphemes (units of meaning). Here is an example of these two approaches with the word 'contradict':   syllable split – con/tra/dict

morpheme split – contra/dict.

As the purpose of this workbook is to teach students about English morphology, this workbook will focus solely on breaking words up into morphemes. The prefix 'contra' means 'against' and the root word 'dict' means 'say'. The student learns that the meaning of the word is 'say against'. When taught this way, the student learns to spell the word on the basis of its meaning. He/she can also begin to make connections to other words with the prefix 'contra': 'contravene', 'contraband' etc. and to the root word 'dict': 'dictate', 'dictator', 'predict' etc. Where a morpheme has a number of meanings, the most common one has been selected. The teacher can add meanings if he/she thinks this will enhance the learning.

This workbook offers a variety of activities to help the student practice and consolidate what has been learned. The teacher can select from the activities to suit the student.

How this workbook is organized

The morphemes in this workbook are grouped loosely into chapters according to their function or meanings. For example, Book 1 introduces common suffixes ('s', 'es', 'ed' and 'ing'). Book 2 introduces common suffixes which change the grammatical function and meaning of words. Book 3 introduces prefixes which mean 'no' or 'wrong' etc.

Below is a chart with the content of this workbook:

Book	Type of morphemes	Morphemes introduced	Teaching focus
1	suffixes	's', 'es', 'ed', 'ing'	plural, past and present tenses
2	suffixes	'ful', 'less', 'ness', 'er', 'est', 'ly', 'en', 'ish', 'y', 'able', 'ible'	suffixes that enhance or change meanings
3	prefixes	'un', 'in', 'im', 'il', 'ir', 'mis', 'dis'	prefixes that mean 'no' or 'wrong'
4	prefixes	're', 'pre', 'post', 'ante', 'anti'	prefixes relating to time or mean 'again'
5	prefixes, base/root words	'uni', 'bi', 'tri', 'quad', 'dec', 'cent', 'multi'	prefixes, base/root words relating to number and quantity
6	prefixes	'sub', 'super', 'trans', 'inter', 'ex'	prefixes relating to prepositions
7	prefixes, root words	'magna'/'magni', 'mega', 'min'/'mini', 'micro'	prefixes, root words relating to size
8	root words	'cap'/'capit', 'man', 'spect', 'ped', 'bio', 'viv'/'vit', 'mort'	root words relating to parts of body, life and death
9	root words	'dict', 'graph', 'scrib'/'script', 'mem'	root words relating to speaking, writing and remembering
10	root words	'ject', 'tract', 'port', 'struct', 'labor', 'fact', 'form'	root words relating to actions

Before using these worksheets

Before using these worksheets, it is important for the teacher to introduce each morpheme orally. He/she can discuss the meaning of the morpheme, asking the students to provide further examples within words and sentences. It is also fun to get the students to create their own words using the morpheme they are studying.

> **Glossary**
>
> **morpheme** – the smallest unit of meaningful language
> **affix** – an addition to a base word which adds or changes the meaning of the word
> **prefix** – an affix that is placed before a base word or another prefix and that changes the meaning of the word
> **suffix** – an affix that is added to the end of a word and that changes its meaning
> **vowel suffix** – a suffix beginning with a vowel, e.g. 'ed', 'ing' and 'able'
> **consonant suffix** – a suffix beginning with a consonant, e.g. 'ful', 'less' and 'ment'
> **base word** – gives the word its basic meaning; prefixes and suffixes are added to base words
> **root word** – a base word that comes from Greek or Latin but has no meaning in English without affixes, e.g. 'ject' in 'reject'.

English spelling is complicated – who's to blame?

Blame the Angles, Saxons and Jutes because they invaded England from the northwest coast of Europe. A mixture of these languages formed Anglo-Saxon. Today, the closest languages to Anglo-Saxon are Frisian, Dutch and German. Many of the most common words in English originate from Anglo-Saxon: 'alive', 'bed', 'hand', 'can', 'cup', 'fish', 'man', 'god', 'game', 'house', 'name' and many more.

400's AD

Blame the Normans because in 1066 they invaded England from Normandy in France. They replaced the English ruling classes with their own aristocracy and the language of government and law was French. For a few centuries, two languages were spoken: French by the rich and powerful ('beef', 'veal', 'mutton', 'pork' and 'venison') and Anglo-Saxon by the common people ('ox', 'cow', 'sheep', 'swine' and 'deer'). By the 14th century, the aristocracy became English and the language of government and literature became English, but many French words remained in the language.

1066 – 1400

Blame the printing press and the Great Vowel Shift. In 1480, William Caxton brought the printing press from Germany to England. This was a communications revolution (a bit like the internet)! London became the center of printing and the London dialect became dominant. Over many years, there was a change in the way English was pronounced. This is called the Great Vowel Shift. The pronunciation of vowels changed and made English more difficult to read. For example, the English used to pronounce the word 'house' – 'hoose'. (They still do in Scotland!) During the Great Vowel Shift, English pronunciation changed to the way we pronounce it today.

1400 – 1700

Blame Shakespeare and the English Renaissance. During the Renaissance, there was an explosion of culture in science, art and literature. This is the time of Shakespeare and Queen Elizabeth I. William Shakespeare coined many new words and expressions that we use to this day. Here are a few: 'knock, knock, who's there?'; 'brave new world'; 'be all and end all'; 'for goodness sake'; 'love is blind'; 'laughing stock'; 'one fell swoop'; 'break the ice'. During the Renaissance, classical (Greek and Roman) civilizations were rediscovered and many Greek and Latin words entered the language.

Shakespeare

1600 – 1700's

Blame the explorers. As a result of their discoveries of new places around the world, new territories were colonized. The English language spread to the British colonies such as America, Canada, Australia, India and parts of Africa. Many new words were brought back from the colonies and entered the language: 'jungle', 'pyjamas' (India), 'banjo' (Africa), 'tattoo' (New Zealand), 'caravan' (Arabic) etc.

1500 – 1945

Blame the industrial revolution because the rapid new technological changes, inventions and products needed new words such as 'train', 'engine', 'pulley', 'combustion', 'electricity', 'telephone', 'telegraph' and 'camera'.

First steam engine
1700 – 1840

Blame Samuel Johnson who wrote the first dictionary in 1755 and fixed the spellings of words in English. Up until that time, people could spell words in different ways. So, he is responsible for the fact that you can only spell a word correctly in one way (and for the spelling lists you get each week)!

Samuel Johnson's dictionary
1755

Blame American English. In the 1820's, Noah Webster published the first American dictionary. He simplified spellings of many English words like 'color' (colour), 'center' (centre) and 'organize' (organise).

After World War II, America and American culture became the most influential in the world. Many American words and phrases are now used by all English speakers today such as: 'sneakers', 'sweater', 'buck' (dollar), 'pants', 'bail', 'hang out', 'lighten up', 'pig out', 'screw up', 'uptight', 'trash' and many more.

1820's – today

And today? Today, many new words are being created to describe fast-developing technologies, such as: 'website', 'surf', 'text', 'selfie', 'email', 'to friend', 'unfriend', 'tweet'.

This rich history has made English a difficult language to read and spell. It has also made it a wonderfully rich language that is used by millions of people across the globe to communicate with one another.

Did you know that English has more words than any other language in the world?

English spellings from Latin, Greek and Anglo-Saxon

We can often indentify the origin of words in English according to their spellings. Here are some examples of how we can tell that words come from Latin, Greek and Anglo-Saxon.

Spellings from Latin

- /sh/ spelled 'ti' ('na<u>ti</u>on'), 'ci' ('ra<u>ci</u>al'), si ('ten<u>si</u>on')
- /ch/ spelled 't' ('for<u>t</u>une' and 'na<u>t</u>ure')
- /s/ spelled 'c' as in '<u>c</u>ity' and '<u>c</u>ertain'
- Many words from Latin are multisyllabic.
- Latin words are simple to read as they have few complex vowel spellings like 'oa', 'igh' and 'ough'.

Spellings from Greek

- /i/ spelled 'y' ('m<u>y</u>th' and 'g<u>y</u>m')
- /ie/ spelled 'y' ('c<u>y</u>cle' and 't<u>y</u>pe')
- /f/ spelled 'ph' ('<u>ph</u>one', 'gra<u>ph</u>' and '<u>ph</u>obia')
- /k/ spelled 'ch' ('s<u>ch</u>ool', '<u>Ch</u>ristmas' and 'monar<u>ch</u>')
- /n/ spelled 'pn' ('<u>pn</u>eumonia')
- /s/ spelled 'ps' ('<u>ps</u>ychology')
- Words ending in 'ic' ('trag<u>ic</u>', 'com<u>ic</u>', 'mus<u>ic</u>')

Spellings from Anglo-Saxon

- double consonants 'ff, 'll', 'ss' ('sni<u>ff</u>', 'sma<u>ll</u>', 'gra<u>ss</u>')
- spellings 'ch' ('<u>ch</u>in', '<u>ch</u>air') and 'th' ('<u>th</u>an', '<u>th</u>ick', '<u>th</u>ank')
- spellings 'k' ('<u>k</u>ind', '<u>k</u>ill', '<u>k</u>ick') and 'ng' ('ri<u>ng</u>', 'sti<u>ng</u>')
- /w/ spelled 'wh' ('<u>wh</u>en', '<u>wh</u>isper') and 'wr' ('<u>wr</u>ite', '<u>wr</u>ist')
- /l/ spelled 'le' ('app<u>le</u>', 'midd<u>le</u>', 'bubb<u>le</u>') in two-syllable words
- Most common high-frequency words come from Anglo-Saxon.

Book 1: 'City of Secrets'

Contents

Book 1: What are morphemes?

Morphemes are parts of the word that give it meaning. The **base word** is the main part. The **prefix** is added to the beginning of the word. A **suffix** is added to the end. Prefixes and suffixes can change the meaning of the word. Learning to identify the parts of the words can help you to understand the word and spell it accurately.

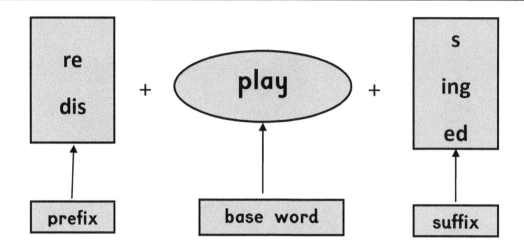

How many words can you make using these morphemes?

_____

_____

_____

_____

_____

_____

_____

_____

_____

_____

_____

Book 1: Base words and suffixes

Morphemes are parts of the word that give it meaning. The **base word** is the main part. A **suffix** is added to the end of the base word. Suffixes can change the meaning of the word. Learning to identify the parts of the words can help you to understand the word and spell it accurately.

help less	freshly	holding	reached	useful	greatest
likely	blinded	selfish	foolish	speaker	opened
lifting	endless	hopeful	darken	joyful	childish
tighten	fighter	neatness	leader	cooking	brainy

Underline the base word in each of the words above. Then break the words up into base word and suffix and write them in the grid below.

	base word	suffix			base word	suffix
1	help	less		13		
2				14		
3				15		
4				16		
5				17		
6				18		
7				19		
8				20		
9				21		
10				22		
11				23		
12				24		

Book 1: Suffixes 's', 'ing' and 'ed'

Suffixes are word endings. Suffixes are important because they can change the meaning of words. The most common suffixes are: **'s'**, **'ing'** and **'ed'**.

Add an 's' to a word like 'flower' – you get 'flower**s**'. The suffix 's' tells us there is more than one flower, e.g. 'I picked a bunch of flowers.' This is called 'plural'.

Add the suffix 'ing' to the word 'jump' – you get 'jump**ing**'. The suffix 'ing' is a verb ending. Here it is used to show an action is happening now, e.g. 'I am jumping now.'

Add the suffix 'ed' to the word 'jump' – you get 'jump**ed**'. The suffix 'ed' tells us that the action happened in the past, e.g. 'I jumped into the water yesterday.'

Add the suffixes **'s'**, **'ed'** and **'ing'** to the words in the text.

Finn was brows_____ in the bazaar, when a tall girl with spiky blonde hair appear_____ by his side. It was Izzy! She was back from her travel_____ with her dad. Kit was under a stall, hunt_____ for climb_____ hook_____. Kit came out from under the stall. He was grasp_____ some rusty hook_____. Just then, a crowd of people began push_____ past them.

"Stop that thief!" a loud voice shout_____. Monk shot out of the crowd and hurl_____ himself into Finn's arms. He was cling_____ to Finn.

"I said grab him!" yell_____ an angry stall keeper. He push_____ his way through the crowd. He was point_____ angrily at Monk.

"He's the thief! You need to pay for what he's been steal_____!"

"He's a monkey!" Finn explain_____. "He doesn't understand. Please, let me pay for it," he plead_____.

"I see Monk is up to his old trick_____," Izzy whisper_____ to Kit.

Kit held out a clutch of batter_____ note_____ to the angry man.

Book 1: Suffixes 's' and 'es'

When you add an 's' to a noun, it shows there is more than one thing. For example, add 's' to the base word 'book' – you get 'book**s**'. This is called 'plural'. Sometimes, the sound at the end of a word makes it hard to add an 's' sound so we have to add '**es**'.

Spelling tip: If the base word ends with the sounds 's', 'x', 'ch', 'sh' or 'z' – add 'es'.

Underline the last sound in the word. Then add 's' or 'es' accordingly.

cat s__

frog___

dish___

stitch___

kiss___

bench___

wish___

batch___

winter___

ranch___

coat___

box___

sock___

watch___

step___

punch___

computer___

buzz___

Add 's' or 'es' and change the nouns to plural.

Kit was looking for hooks in the box____ under the stall. He found batch____ of hooks for climbing. Izzy led them to an old, musty shop. It seemed as if treasure and rich____ were hidden in the dusty box____ on the shelves and under the bench____. When they reached the old shop, a man stepped out of the shadow____. He looked at them through thick reading glass____. He looked at the necklace. His eye____ were glued on it, fearfully.

"Servant____ of the old sorcerer are seeking this," he said. Just then, a hooded figure leaped down from the rafter____. He landed inch____ away from Finn. There were smash____ and crash____ as the figure fell against the heavy bookcase.

"Run! Follow the direction____ to the old town. The answer____ you seek are in the ruin____ of the old museum," hissed the old shopkeeper. They raced along the street____ and alleyway____.

Book 1: Adding the suffix 's' to words ending in 'y'

Adding the suffix 's' to a noun shows there is more than one thing. For example, add 's' to the base word 'book' – you get 'book**s**'. This is called 'plural'.

Spelling tips:

1. If the base word ends in 'ay', 'ey', 'oy' or 'uy', just add 's'.
   For example: to<u>y</u> + s = toy**s**

2. If the letter before the 'y' at the end of word is a consonant, change the 'y' to 'i' and add the suffix 'es'. For example: ba<u>b</u>y + s = bab**ies**

Underline the last two letters in the word. Change the words to plural by adding the correct suffix.

ba<u>by</u>	<u>babies</u>	story	_____
tr<u>ay</u>	_____	buddy	_____
lady	_____	bay	_____
day	_____	puppy	_____
party	_____	day	_____
mummy	_____	country	_____
jelly	_____	monkey	_____
boy	_____	essay	_____
candy	_____	family	_____
valley	_____	survey	_____
cherry	_____	beauty	_____
joy	_____	memory	_____
journey	_____	decoy	_____
play	_____	donkey	_____

Book 1: The three sounds of the suffix 'ed'

The suffix '**ed**' is added to the end of verbs to show that an action has happened in the past. For example: the verb 'walk' in the past tense is 'walk<u>ed</u>'.

The suffix '**ed**' can spell three sounds: /**t**/ as in the word 'jump<u>ed</u>'

/**d**/ as in the word 'lon<u>ged</u>'

/**id**/ as in the word 'want<u>ed</u>'

Despite sounding three different ways, the suffix 'ed' is always spelled 'ed'.

Read the text below and highlight the words with the suffix 'ed'. Listen to the sound at the end of the words. Write the words in the correct column.

Finn pulled the strange-looking necklace from his pouch. It looked battered and damaged. The metal was dented. Izzy reached out to touch it.

"Lovely junk!" snorted Kit. "Finn's mom will just throw it away!" He glanced at it. "It has only one jewel left in it!" he mocked and handed it to Izzy. Izzy lifted the necklace and gazed at it. She rubbed the dust off with her fingers. She stared at it. "You're wrong. This is real amber," she announced.

/t/	/d/	/id/
	pulled	

Now choose two words from each box and write a sentence with them in your book.

Book 1: Adding the suffix 'ed' (doubling)

The suffix 'ed' indicates that the action has taken place in the past. Sometimes we must double the last consonant when adding 'ed' to the base word.

For example: 'hop' – 'ho**pp**ed'. This happens in one-syllable words where the vowel next to the last consonant is a 'short vowel' (/a/, /e/, /i/, /o/, /u/). For example: 'p<u>a</u>t' – 'patted'; 'b<u>e</u>g' – 'begged'; 't<u>i</u>p' – 'tipped'; 'n<u>o</u>d' – 'nodded'; 'h<u>u</u>g' – 'hugged'. If the short vowel is not next to the last consonant, as in 'jump', just add 'ed': 'jumped'.

If the vowel sound next to the last consonant sound is a long vowel sound, as in 'n<u>ee</u>d', or 'p<u>oa</u>ch', just add 'ed': 'needed', 'poached'.

Add the suffix 'ed' to the words in the chart below. Underline the vowel spelling. Is it next to the last consonant? Is it a short or long vowel sound? Should you double the last consonant?

Underline the vowel spelling	Is it next to the last consonant?	Is it a short vowel sound?	Double?	+ ed
t<u>a</u>p	✓	✓	✓	tapped
wag				
mend				
lift				
help				
trip				
reach				
pluck				
moan				
peel				
drag				
print				

Book 1: Adding the suffixes 'ed' and 'ing'

The suffix '**ed**' indicates that the action has taken place in the past. Here, the suffix '**ing**' shows that the action is taking place in the present. Sometimes we must double the last consonant when adding 'ed' or 'ing' to the base word.
For example: 'h<u>o</u>p' – 'ho**pp**ed' and 'ho**pp**ing'

This happens in one–syllable words where the vowel next to the last consonant is a short vowel sound (/a/, /e/, /i/, /o/, /u/).

If the short vowel sound is not next to the last consonant, just add 'ed' or 'ing'.
For example: 'j<u>u</u>mp' – 'jumped' and 'jumping'

If the vowel sound next to the last consonant sound is a long vowel sound, just add 'ed' or 'ing'.
For example: 'r<u>ea</u>ch' – 'reached' and 'reaching'

Add the suffix 'ed' to the words in the chart below. Underline the vowel spelling in the word. Is it next to the last consonant? Is it a short or long vowel sound? Should you double the last consonant?

Underline the vowel spelling	Is it next to the last consonant?	Is it a short vowel sound?	Double?	+ ed	+ ing
r<u>i</u>p	✓	✓	✓	ripped	ripping
huff					
plot					
help					
mend					
drip					
groan					
press					
brag					
slam					

Book 1: Suffix 'ed' – cloze activity (highlighted vowels)

Add the suffix 'ed' to the words in the text. The vowel spellings have been highlighted for you. Do you need to double the last consonant before adding 'ed'?

They ran along the streets. Izzy scan_ned_ the directions. Kit and Finn follow____ her into a maze of alleyways. Monk clutch____ Finn's shoulder. They look____ behind them as they ran. A shadow flit____ across the dark alley.

"He's coming!" gasp____ Izzy. Her face was twist____ in panic. They press____ themselves into a dark doorway.

"It's getting late!" pant____ Kit. He squint____ upwards.

"We'd better keep jumping across the rooftops!" he said. This fill____ Izzy with dread.

"Please, Iz." Kit want____ to reassure her.
They slip____ through a door and sprint____ up a flight of stairs. They ran along the rooftops and hop____ from one rooftop to another.

Suddenly, they stop____ at a big gap between the buildings. Izzy's face was screw____ up with fear.

Book 1: Suffix 'ed' – cloze activity

Add the suffix 'ed' to the words in the text. Do you need to double the last consonant before adding 'ed'?

They ran along the streets. Izzy scan_ned_ the directions. Kit and Finn follow____ her into a maze of alleyways. Monk clutch____ Finn's shoulder. They look____ behind them as they ran. A shadow flit_____ across the dark alley.

"He's coming!" gasp____ Izzy. Her face was twist____ in panic. They press____ themselves into a dark doorway.

"It's getting late!" pant____ Kit. He squint____ upwards.

"We'd better keep jumping across the rooftops!" he said. This fill____ Izzy with dread.

"Please, Iz." Kit want____ to reassure her. They slip____ through a door and sprint____ up a flight of stairs. They ran along the rooftops and hop____ from one rooftop to another.

Suddenly, they stop____ at a big gap between the buildings. Izzy's face was screw____ up with fear.

Book 1: Suffixes 'ed' and 'ing'

Now apply the same principles as on page 14 and add the suffixes 'ed' and 'ing' to the words in the chart below. Underline the vowel spellings. Is it a short vowel? Is it next to the last consonant?

base word	short vowel?	double?	+ ed	+ ing
jog	✓	✓	jogged	jogging
peel				
beg				
tip				
help				
plan				
chop				
blink				
pick				
flap				
jump				
wag				
play				
skip				
shop				
mend				
rap				

Book 1: Adding 'ed' and 'ing' to words ending in vowels

When you add the suffixes 'ed' and 'ing' to a base word that ends with a vowel, you drop the 'e' at the end of the base word:

For example: bake + **ed** = baked

bake + **ing** = baking

The suffixes 'ed' and 'ing' are called 'vowel suffixes' because they begin with a vowel.

Add the suffixes 'ed' and 'ing' to these base words.

base word	drop the e?	+ ed	+ ing
dive	✓	dived	diving
reach			
phone			
hate			
walk			
use			
live			
race			
hope			
hike			
bounce			
like			
dance			
frame			
train			
arrange			

Book 1: Adding suffixes 'ing' and 'ed'

Help this confused cyclops add the suffixes 'ing' and 'ed' to the base words below.

wave + ing =   <u>waving</u>   wave + ed =   <u>waved</u>

crack + ing = _____   crack + ed = _____

blame + ing = _____   blame + ed = _____

brag + ing = _____   brag + ed = _____

drop + ing = _____   drop + ed = _____

vote + ing = _____   vote + ed = _____

hope + ing = _____   hope + ed = _____

hop + ing = _____   hop + ed = _____

mend + ing = _____   mend + ed = _____

chase + ing = _____   chase + ed = _____

tap + ing = _____   tap + ed = _____

tape + ing = _____   tape + ed = _____

delete + ing = _____   delete + ed = _____

punch + ing = _____   punch + ed = _____

Book 1: Vowel and consonant suffixes

A **vowel suffix** starts with a vowel. For example: '**ed**' and '**ing**'.

When you add a vowel suffix to a base word that ends with a vowel, you drop the 'e' at the end of the base word.

For example: bak~~e~~ + ing = baking
bak~~e~~ + ed = baked

A **consonant suffix** starts with a consonant. For example: '**less**' and '**ful**'.

When you add a consonant suffix, keep the 'e' at the end of the base word.

For example: use + less = useless

Underline the first letter of the suffix. Now add the suffix to the base word.

us~~e~~ + <u>i</u>ng = _using_

use + ed = _____

use + ful = _____

use + less = _____

use + er = _____

hope + ing = _____

hope + ed = _____

hope + ful = _____

hope + less = _____

like + ing = _____

like + ed = _____

like + ly = _____

shame + ing = _____

shame + ed = _____

shame + ful = _____

shame + less = _____

amuse + ing = _____

amuse + ed = _____

amuse + ment = _____

care + ing = _____

care + ed = _____

care + ful = _____

care + less = _____

care + er = _____

Book 1: Suffix 'ed' – cloze activity

Add 'ed' to the words below. Read the words and then insert them in the text.

gaze___	open___	arrive___	pulse___
grab___	spot___	waste__	stop___
clamber__	lower___	appear__	explore__

They looked down into the gloomy space below. Kit got his rope and threaded it into a hook in the wall. They _____ themselves down one by one.

"This is the courtyard of the ancient museum! We've _____ exactly where we need to be," said Kit.

They _____ the dim corridor. Soon they _____ at a heavy wooden door. It _____ into a huge hall.

Izzy _____ Finn's arm. "Look, it's a map of an ancient kingdom. My father has talked about it for years!"

They _____ at it in amazement. The amber jewel glowed and _____ more brightly. It lit up the hall.

Suddenly, they saw a statue of a warrior holding a sword.

Finn _____ a purple orb in the warrior's hand.

Kit _____ no time and _____ up the statue's arm.

Just then, the door flung open. A cyclops _____ in the doorway.

Book 1: Adding vowel and consonant suffixes – in text

ing		less
ed		ful

Add the suffixes 'ing', 'ed', 'less' and 'ful' to the base words.

Kit clamber____ up the statue's arm. He was care____ not to fall. He inch____ closer to the purple orb. He tried to prise it loose use____ his climbing hook, but it was use____!

Suddenly, the door open____. A frighten____ cyclops appear____ in the lit doorway. It glare____ crazily from one bloodshot eye in the middle of its forehead. It looked hate____.

At its side was a face____ hooded spy! The cyclops was be____ controlled by the hood____ spy. The cyclops lunge____ across the room. It attack____ the stone statue with a massive stone hammer.

The statue was break____ up. Shards of rock rain____ down to the ground. The statue's stone arm crumble____ and collapse____. The purple orb tumble____ to the ground. Izzy race____ to grab it as it fell. Kit was stuck on the statue. He felt help____. He fell off as it explode____ into a cloud of dust. Izzy retreat____ into the shadows.

Finn hand____ Monk the amber necklace. "Take it to Izzy," he whisper____ to Monk. "Follow me! I have the orb!" he yelled to the cyclops. The cyclops blunder____ this way and that, swing____ its hammer with fury. Kit lay gasp____ in the dust. He stagger____ to his feet and lunge____ at the hood____ spy.

Book 1: Adding 'ed' to base words ending in 'y'

When a base word ends in the spellings '**ay**', '**ey**' or '**oy**', just add the suffix 'ed'.

For example: pl**ay** + ed = played

If there is a consonant before the 'y', change the 'y' to 'i'.

For example: car**ry** + ed = carr**i**ed

Add the suffix 'ed' to the words in the chart.

base word	ends in ay, ey, oy?	has consonant before y?	change y to i?	+ ed
wor**r**y	✗	✓	✓	worried
copy				
study				
stay				
deny				
hurry				
employ				
envy				
marry				
rely				
betray				
fancy				
delay				
tidy				

Book 1: Adding 'ed' and 'ing' to words ending in 'y'

When a base word ends in the spellings '**ay**', '**ey**' or '**oy**', just add the suffix 'ed'.

For example: pl**ay** + ed = played

If there is a consonant before the 'y', change the 'y' to 'i'.

For example: car**ry** + ed = carr**i**ed

BUT

When you add the suffix '**ing**' to base words ending in 'y', just add 'ing' to the base word.

For example: carry + ing = carrying

Add the suffixes 'ed' and 'ing' to the words in the chart.

base word	+ ed	+ ing	base word	+ ed	+ ing
copy	copied	copying	dry		
marry			sway		
study			empty		
play			reply		
hurry			worry		
try			rally		
carry			decay		
enjoy			obey		
bury			pray		
bully			rely		
cry			delay		
lobby			defy		

Book 1: Adding 'ed' and 'ing' to multi–syllabic words

To add the suffixes 'ed' and 'ing' to multi–syllable base words that have a short vowel before the last consonant, you first need to identify which syllable in the word is stressed.

If the stress is on the first syllable, like in the word 'credit', you just add the suffix: cred it + ed = cred ited   or   cred it + ing = cred iting

If the stress is on the final syllable, like in the word 'regret', you must double the last consonant: regret + ed = regretted   or   regret + ing = regretting

Say the word aloud and underline the stressed syllable. Do you need to double the last consonant? Now add the suffixes 'ed' and 'ing'.

stressed syllable	double last consonant?	+ ed	+ ing
regret	✓	regretted	regretting
profit	✗		
limit			
admit			
rebel			
omit			
commit			
exit			
acquit			
visit			
target			
permit			
equip			

Book 1: Revision 1: suffixes 's', 'es', 'ed' and 'ing'

Add the suffixes to the base words below. Remember the spelling tips you have learned.

	base word	add suffix	spelling		base word	add suffix	spelling
1	book	s	books	16	ash	s	
2	fox	s	foxes	17	enter	ed	
3	open	ed		18	baby	s	
4	reach	ed		19	fine	ed	
5	hope	ed		20	face	ing	
6	hop	ed		21	sit	ing	
7	take	ing		22	tap	ed	
8	lap	ing		23	tape	ed	
9	carry	ing		24	deny	ing	
10	lady	s		25	save	ing	
11	toy	s		26	hobby	s	
12	cry	ing		27	hurry	ed	
13	open	ing		28	dry	ing	
14	handle	ed		29	have	ing	
15	try	ed		30	stop	ed	

Correct your errors here:

_____

_____

Book 1: Revision 2: suffixes 's', 'es', 'ed' and 'ing'

Add the suffixes to the base words below. Remember the spelling tips you have learned.

	base word	add suffix	spelling		base word	add suffix	spelling
1	lamp	s		16	punch	s	
2	brush	s		17	foster	ed	
3	suffer	ed		18	cherry	s	
4	free	ed		19	tune	ed	
5	hike	ed		20	chase	ing	
6	plot	ed		21	drop	ing	
7	save	ing		22	dot	ed	
8	flap	ing		23	dote	ed	
9	dry	ing		24	multiply	ing	
10	poppy	s		25	place	ing	
11	activity	s		26	nappy	s	
12	fry	ing		27	pity	ed	
13	please	ing		28	supply	ing	
14	stumble	ed		29	cope	ing	
15	pry	ed		30	drag	ed	

Correct your errors here:

_____

_____

Book 2: 'The Bones of Ruin'

Contents

Book 2: Suffixes 'ful' and 'less'

The suffix 'ful' means 'full of', as in the word 'fear**ful**' (full of fear). Note that this suffix is spelled with only one 'l'.

The suffix 'less' means 'without', as in the word 'fear**less**' (without fear).

When these suffixes are added to the base word, they change a noun into an adjective. For example: I have a <u>fear</u> of the dark. (noun)

The <u>fearful</u> child hid under the bed. (adjective)

The <u>fearless</u> hero fought the dragon. (adjective)

Complete the phrases with a suitable noun.

A helpful	_waiter_	A headless	_monster_
A hopeful	_____	A cloudless	_____
A useful	_____	A ruthless	_____
A restful	_____	A beardless	_____
A careful	_____	A careless	_____
A harmful	_____	A spotless	_____
A spiteful	_____	A treeless	_____
A joyful	_____	A homeless	_____
A fearful	_____	A tuneless	_____
A forgetful	_____	A fruitless	_____
A colorful	_____	An endless	_____
A successful	_____	A sleeveless	_____

Can you add the suffixes 'ful' or 'less' to the base words **'cheer'**, **'tact'**, **'pain'** and **'mind'**? Discuss the meaning of these new words and write a sentence for each one.

Book 2: Suffixes 'ful' and 'less'

The suffix 'ful' means 'full of', as in the word 'fear**ful**' (full of fear). Note that this suffix is spelled with only one 'l'.

The suffix 'less' means 'without', as in the word 'fear**less**' (without fear).

When these suffixes are added to the base word, they change a noun into an adjective. For example: I have a <u>fear</u> of the dark. (noun)

The <u>fear**ful**</u> child hid under the bed. (adjective)

The <u>fear**less**</u> hero fought the dragon. (adjective)

Cut out the boxes and match up the two parts of the sentences so that they make sense.

The play<u>ful</u> puppy	lost her glasses.
The mother<u>less</u> orphan	chased the stick.
The forget<u>ful</u> granny	had no family.
The moon<u>less</u> night	visited the haunted house.
The grace<u>ful</u> dancer	poisoned the water.
The head<u>less</u> ghost	means endless energy.
The harm<u>ful</u> chemical	was so dark we got lost.
Limit<u>less</u> energy	took her final bow.

Now make up your own 5 words using the suffixes 'ful' or 'less'. Write a sentence in your book for each of the words.

Book 2: Suffixes 'ful' and 'less'

Add the suffixes 'ful' and 'less' to the base words in the text. Then reread the text to make sure it makes sense.

The three friends rode across the moonlit sky on the back of the winged Guardian. They were not afraid. They were fear_____ as they looked down to the wonder_____ valley below.

The creature introduced himself. "I am a Griffin. You have released me from my prison in the purple orb. That orb in your pocket, Izzy, contains power_____ magic.

"The ancient kingdom was once kept safe by ten Guardians. Each had their own immense power. A hate_____ sorcerer yearned to control them. He wanted limit_____ power all for himself. He used the magic orb to imprison the Guardians in ten amber jewels. He inserted the jewels into a price_____ necklace. Now the trapped Guardians were power_____ and help_____, but he was not completely success_____. He was care_____. Before he could harness the Guardians' power, there was a mighty explosion. The amber jewels were scattered across the land. Only one jewel was left in the necklace. All was not hope_____. Friends of the Guardians searched for them. They were tire_____. When they found the Guardians, they built wonder_____ monuments around them to protect them. Your quest is to find the remaining nine monuments and release the grate_____ Guardians."

Book 2: Suffix 'ness'

When the suffix 'ness' is added to an adjective base word, it changes the word into a noun. For example:

adjective	noun

good + ness = goodness

This noun is an abstract noun because you can't touch it or see it.

Spelling tip: When the base word ends in 'n', as in the word 'mean', you will spell it like this:

mean + ness = mea**nn**ess

Add the suffix 'ness' to the base words and insert them into the text below.

forgive_____	kind_____	green_____	tired_____	wicked_____
sick_____	deaf_____	neat_____	bright_____	fit_____

1. _____ is a major cause of car accidents.
2. She showed her _____ by visiting the old lady every week.
3. As the plot develops, the reader realizes the true _____ of the sorcerer's plan.
4. We shielded our eyes from the _____ of the sun.
5. The football coach said that _____ was essential for all sportsmen and women.
6. After the trial, the criminal asked the victim for _____.
7. During spring, one can see the _____ of the new leaves on the trees.
8. The child on the boat suffered from sea _____.
9. After tidying up, he showed his mom the _____ of his room.
10. During the war, the explosion of a bomb caused his _____.

Book 2: Suffixes 'ful', 'less' and 'ness'

Add the suffixes 'ful' or 'less' to the words below. Then write the whole word. Then insert the correct words in the sentences.

base word	suffix	suffix	
care	less	ness	carelessness (not taking care)
cheer		ness	(state of happiness)
self		ness	(thinking of others, not ones
use		ness	(being useful)
forget		ness	(state of poor memory)
thought		ness	(being inconsiderate)
home		ness	(state of having no home)

1. In the big cities, there is a serious problem of _____.

2. Nan was getting worried about her _____.

3. Dan called the dog, but he ran off. Rover was showing his _____.

4. The man risked his life for the child. It was an act of _____.

5. Greg forgot his mom's birthday. This was a result of his _____.

6. The man dropped the glass bowl. This was just _____.

7. The doctor said that Jan's _____ was helping her get better.

Now add the suffixes 'ful' or 'less' and 'ness' to the base words **'sleep'**, **'tune'**, **'power'** and **'fear'**. Write a sentence for each word.

Book 2: Adding suffixes to words ending in 'y'

The suffixes 'ful', 'less' and 'ness' are consonant suffixes (they begin with a consonant). Just add them to a base word. For example:

arm + ful = armful   use + less = useless   fresh + ness = freshness

Spelling tips:

1. When the base word ends with 'y', change the 'y' to 'i'.
   For example: beauty + ful = beautiful   silly + ness = silliness

2. When the base word ending in 'y' has only one syllable, keep the 'y'.
   For example: dry + ness = dryness

Add the suffixes to the base words. Do you need to change the 'y' to 'i'?

beauty + ful = __beautiful__

spine + less = _____

clumsy + ness =_____

rest + ful = _____

blame + less = _____

nasty + ness = _____

plenty + ful = _____

word + less = _____

pity + less = _____

hard + ness = _____

force + ful = _____

body + less = _____

lonely + ness = _____

time + less = _____

happy + ness = _____

duty + ful = _____

empty + ness = _____

mouth + ful = _____

sight + less = _____

holy + ness = _____

shy + ness = _____

aim + less = _____

brim + ful = _____

thought + less =_____

lazy + ness = _____

sleepy + ness = _____

wish + ful = _____

bossy + ness = _____

Book 2: Suffixes 'er' and 'est'

When the suffix 'er' is added to an adjective, it means 'more'.

adjective

For example: sweet + er = sweet**er**

When the suffix 'est' is added to an adjective, it means 'the most'.

adjective

For example: sweet + est = sweet**est**

Add the suffixes 'er' and 'est' to the base words.

hard + er = _harder_	hard + est = _hardest_
cold + er = _____	cold + est = _____
old + er = _____	old + est = _____
cheap + er = _____	cheap + est = _____
high + er = _____	high + est = _____
green + er = _____	green + est = _____
fast + er = _____	fast + est = _____

Now insert the correct words into the sentences below.

1. My sister is the _____ in her class. She is two years _____ than me.

2. The brown horse ran _____ than the white one. He was the _____ in the race.

3. January was _____ than December. It was the _____ month of the year.

4. The _____ item in the sale was a belt. The price was _____ than last week.

5. After the rain, the grass was _____ than before. It was the _____ he had ever seen.

6. The six times table is _____ than the five times table. It is the _____ times table we have learned so far.

7. Greg climbed the _____ mountain in Europe. The _____ he climbed, the weaker he became.

Book 2: Suffixes 'er' and 'est'

When the suffix 'er' is added to an adjective, it means 'more'.

adjective

For example: sweet + er = sweet<u>er</u>

When the suffix 'est' is added to an adjective, it means 'the most'.

adjective

For example: sweet + est = sweet<u>est</u>

Spelling tips: The suffixes 'er' and 'est' are vowel suffixes. Remember to:
1. double the last consonant if there is a 'short vowel' in front of it
2. drop the 'e' if the base word ends in an 'e'
3. change the 'y' to 'i' if the base word ends in a 'y'.

Add the suffixes 'er' and 'est' to the base words.

base word	double?	drop e?	change y to i?	+ er	+ est
big	✓			bigger	biggest
funny			✓	funnier	funniest
fine		✓			
heavy					
large					
kind					
cheap					
happy					
hot					
thin					
safe					
sad					
silly					

Now add the suffixes 'er' and 'est' to the words: **'lazy'**, **'strange'**, **'quiet'**, **'wet'**.
Write a sentence for each new word.

Book 2: Suffixes 'er' and 'est'

Add the suffixes 'er' and 'est' to the base words in the text. Then reread the text to make sure it makes sense.

Finn squinted up at the paint marks on a number of old buildings. "The map is likely to be in the big_____ building. I wonder if these symbols can help us?"

Monk scampered fearlessly into the mist. He gestured eagerly for them to follow him. The sun rose high_____ and the mists began to clear. Monk led them down the narrow_____ of alleyways to a paved clearing. "Welcome to the center of town!" grinned Kit. "Surely the map will be here," he said, pointing to the tall_____ ruin in the square. It was the town hall. Kit began to scale the crumbling staircase. Suddenly, a huge section of staircase crashed to the ground. This was tricky_____ and risky_____ than he had thought. He swung his climbing ax wildly. Luckily, it took hold on an ancient stone. He was the lucky_____ boy in the world!

"I'm OK!" he called down. "Tread carefully! The staircase won't last much long_____. The three inched slowly up the remains of the staircase. It was scary_____ than Izzy had expected. In fact, it was the scary_____ climb of her life! At last, they reached a balcony high up on the outside of the town hall. The early morning sun was getting hot_____. Vines hung from the building. "These vines are strong_____ and safe_____ than the stone staircase. We can climb down with them," said Kit.

Book 2: Suffix 'ly'

When the suffix 'ly' is added to an adjective, it becomes an adverb.

adjective   adverb

slow + ly = slowly

An adverb is a word that tells us how an action is performed. For example:

The boy ate his ice cream. How did he eat his ice cream?

The boy ate his ice cream <u>slowly</u>.

Complete the phrases below.

to eat	<u>hungrily</u>
to run	_____
to think	_____
to sleep	_____
to drive	_____
to write	_____
to dance	_____
to speak	_____
to pray	_____
to listen	_____
to sit	_____
to fight	_____

to <u>play</u>	roughly
to _____	noisily
to _____	happily
to _____	carefully
to _____	softly
to _____	lazily
to _____	elegantly
to _____	fiercely
to _____	tightly
to _____	politely
to _____	bravely
to _____	rudely

Now add the suffix 'ly' to the base words '**clever**', '**quiet**', '**bright**' and '**neat**'. Discuss the meaning of these new words and write a sentence for each one.

Book 2: Add suffix 'ly' to base words ending in 'y'

When the suffix 'ly' is added to an adjective, it becomes an adverb.

adjective	adverb

slow + ly = slowly

Spelling tips:

1. If the base word ends in 'y', change the 'y' to 'i' and add the suffix 'ly'.
   For example: speedy + ly = speed<u>i</u>ly

2. If the word already has a suffix, just add 'ly'.
   For example: careful + ly = carefu<u>ll</u>y   normal + ly = norma<u>ll</u>y

Add the suffix 'ly' to the adjectives below and turn them into adverbs.

to rest laz~~y~~ily___

to wish hopeful<u>ly</u>___

to think careful_____

to rush excited_____

to drink thirsty _____

to wave cheerful_____

to fight aggressive_____

to speak soft_____

to dress elegant_____

to eat greedy_____

to act foolish_____

to lose bad_____

to shout angry_____

to worry frantical_____

to trip clumsy_____

to work busy_____

to behave normal_____

to crawl creepy_____

to regret sad_____

to point sharp_____

to fight brave_____

to finish easy_____

to miss narrow_____

to hug tight_____

Now choose five phrases from the lists above and write a sentence for each phrase. You can write the sentence in the past tense. For example: 'He ate his food greedily.'

Book 2: Suffix 'ly'

Choose the suitable base words and insert them into the text. Add the suffix 'ly'. Then reread the text to make sure it makes sense.

Finn and Kit began to scramble (careful/careless) _carefully_ down the building. They swung more (coward/adventurous) _____ as they realized the tough ladders of vines could hold their weight. Izzy paused and glanced (fearful/fearless) _____ behind her. Was that a shadowy figure watching them? They landed (insecure/safe) _____ beside a row of old shops. Dusty boxes were piled (neat/haphazard) _____ in the windows.

"The fountain is that way," said Kit (urgent/patient) _____.

"Wait a second! This is a bookshop. You often find maps in bookshops!" cried Izzy (excited/angry) _____. Kit leaned his shoulder against the door. It opened (smooth/creaky) _____. Izzy squeezed (careful/aggressive) _____ through the narrow gap. (Sudden/Slow) _____, Izzy's face appeared in the cracked window.

"I've got it!" she called (sad/cheerful) _____, waving a wad of yellowed paper. "The map!" The map opened (stiff/easy) _____ as if not quite ready to share its secrets. It was the same map they had seen on the wall of the old museum. (Fine/Rough) _____ drawn ink drawings clearly showed the position of all the remaining Guardians. Finn looked (distant/close) _____ at the map. He tapped his finger (thoughtful/thoughtless) _____ as he started to piece it all together.

Book 2: Suffix 'en'

When the suffix 'en' is added to an adjective, it changes the word into a verb. For example:

| adjective | $\longrightarrow$ | verb |

short + en = shorten

Its meaning is 'to make' or 'to become'. For example, the word 'shorten' means 'to make shorter'.

Spelling tip: 'en' is a vowel suffix. Don't forget to drop the 'e' if the word ends in an 'e' and double the last consonant where necessary.

Add the suffix 'en' to the base words and insert them into the text below.

weak_en_   glad_____   wide_____   straight_____   tough_____

quick_____   stiff_____   flat_____   loose_____   worse_____

Complete the opposite sentences below.

Shorten the rope.   --------▶ _Lengthen_ the rope.

Tighten the knot.   _____ the knot.

Strengthen the building.   _____ the building.

Soften the texture.   _____ the texture.

Lighten the room.   _____ the room.

Complete the sentences below.

1. The tunnel was too narrow. We had to _____ it.
2. The fruit was not ready to pick. It had to _____ in the sun.
3. The color was too dark. We had to _____ it.
4. The tea was bitter, so we had to _____ it with sugar.
5. The party was too noisy. The children were told to _____ down.
6. His muscles were weak, so he did exercise to _____ them.

Book 2: Suffix 'ish'

When the suffix 'ish' is added to a base word, it can have different meanings:

green + ish = greenish – means 'a bit green'

girl + ish = girlish – means 'like a girl'

Scot + ish = Scottish – means 'belonging to Scotland'

Spelling tip: 'ish' is a vowel suffix so don't forget to double the last consonant when necessary and drop the 'e' when the base word ends in 'e'.

Add the suffix 'ish' to the base words and match the words to their meaning.

fool + ish =   _foolish_   sensitive to being tickled

freak + ish =   _____   self-centred

Fin + ish =   _____   silly

baby + ish =   _____   slow-moving

tickle + ish =   _____   unusual

slug + ish =   _____   immature

self + ish =   _____   elegant

style + ish =   _____   coming from Finland

Complete the sentences below. Use the words above.

1. The boy didn't have friends because he was _____.
2. Last year, the weather was _____. It rained for a month.
3. He couldn't get out of bed. He felt tired and _____.
4. She couldn't stop laughing because she was so _____.
5. Her clothes were second hand, but she still looked _____.
6. He has come from Finland. He is _____.
7. Mom said that I should grow up and stop being _____.
8. The _____ man gambled away all his money.

44

Book 2: Suffix 'y'

The suffix 'y' changes a noun or a verb to an adjective.

For example:

noun   adjective

1. (noun): hair + y = hairy – The hairy monster fell to the ground.

verb   adjective

2. (verb): sleep + y = sleepy – The sleepy boy did not wake up.

Spelling tips: 'y' is a vowel suffix. Don't forget to double the last consonant and drop the 'e' where necessary.

Add the suffix 'y' to the base words to make adjectives.

Noun ⟶ adjective	Verb ⟶ adjective
bag + y = baggy	taste + y = tasty
air + y =	jump + y =
bone + y =	run + y =
skin + y =	cuddle + y =
fog + y =	curl + y =
cheese + y =	bounce + y =
spice + y =	chop + y =
leaf + y =	giggle + y =
fun + y =	shine + y =
noise + y =	itch + y =
ice + y =	leak + y =

Now choose the best adjectives from above to describe these nouns. Write them in your book: nose, bed, curry, forest, joke, winter, shoes, bear, jeans, body.

This sheet may be photocopied by the purchaser. © Phonic Books Ltd 2019

45

Book 2: Suffixes 'en', 'ish' and 'y'

Add the suffixes 'en', 'ish' and 'y' to the base words in the text. Then reread the text to make sure it makes sense.

Suddenly, two scare_____ things happened. A chilling scream filled the air. At the same moment, a black or dark_____ figure burst through a nearby shop window in a cloud of splintered glass and dust. A spook_____ dark spy! He had been following them all along. Still screaming, he raced towards the fountain.

The three friends felt their pulses quick_____. The fountain was suddenly shrouded in a haze_____, blue_____ light.

Finn felt his throat tight_____. "That spiral of rock shards around the fountain – it's moving!" The white rocks assembled into creep_____ skeleton warriors. Grayish and white_____ skulls glistened in the light as the freak_____ monsters stumbled towards them.

"We have to distract them!" yelled Finn. Grabbing two handfuls of small_____ pebbles, he darted forward. "Here my bone_____ friends, over here!" he bellowed. He scattered the pebbles wildly so the noise would confuse them. The tribe of brute_____ skeleton warriors froze for a second. They were confused by Finn's voice as it echoed off the buildings around them. They turned slowly, raising their sharp_____ed axes.

This sheet may be photocopied by the purchaser. © Phonic Books Ltd 2019

Book 2: Suffix 'able'

The suffix 'able' comes from Latin and French and means 'able to' or 'fit for'. It is very common, as in the words 'readable' or 'comfortable'.

It changes the verb 'adore' into the adjective 'adorable'.
For example: 'That puppy is adorable.'

Add the suffix 'able' to the base words and match the words to their meaning.

accept + able = <u>acceptable</u>   capable of being broken

break + able = _____   stylish

adapt + able = _____   able to be tolerated

prefer + able = _____   cheap enough to buy

afford + able = _____   able to be transferred

pay + able = _____   able to adjust

transfer + able = _____   to be paid, due

fashion + able = _____   more suitable, better

Complete the sentences below. Use the words above.

1. We waited until the price of the tablet became _____.
2. The teacher said the student's behavior was un_____.
3. The athlete knew that the Olympic record was _____.
4. Her clothes were second-hand, but she still looked _____.
5. The animals that survived the meteor crash were _____.
6. The library fine is _____ by the end of the month.
7. The coach said that the football player was _____.
8. Which is _____: reading books or playing video games?

Now make up 5 words with the suffix 'able' and write a sentence for each one.

Book 2: Suffix 'able'

The suffix 'able' comes from Latin and French. It means 'able to be' or 'fit for'.
This suffix changes the **verb** 'adore' into the **adjective** 'adorable'.
For example: 'That puppy is adorable.'

The suffix 'able' is a vowel suffix (it begins with a vowel). When adding it to a word that ends with 'e', like 'excite', you will need to drop the 'e':

excite + able = excitable

Spelling tips:
1. When the base word ends with the spelling 'ge' sounding 'j', or 'ce' sounding 's', keep the 'e'. For example: manage + able = manageable.
2. When the base word ends in 'y', change the 'y' to 'i' when you add this suffix: rely + able = reliable.

Break the word up into base word and suffix. Then explain the meaning.

word	base word	suffix	word meaning
noticeable	notice	able	can be noticed
deniable			
believable			
changeable			
traceable			
knowledgeable			
justifiable			
desirable			
movable			

Add the suffix 'able' to the words below. Remember the spelling tips!

deceiveable   comply_____   service_____   retrieve_____

pronounce_____   remove_____   excuse_____

multiply_____   value_____   unbelieve_____   advise_____

Now choose 5 words and write a sentence for each word.

This sheet may be photocopied by the purchaser. © Phonic Books Ltd 2019

Book 2: Suffix 'ible'

The suffix 'ible' means and sounds the same as the suffix 'able'. It comes from Latin and is often fixed onto Latin root words.

For example: 'cred' (believe) + 'ible' (able to) = 'credible' (believable). It is less common than the suffix 'able'.

Fill in the missing letters and match the words to their correct meanings.

horrible   __horrible____   able to be done or achieved

p__ssible   _____   fit to be eaten

au__ible   _____   able to be reached

v__sible   _____   likely to cause horror

fl__xible   _____   having or showing good sense

acc__ssible   _____   able to be heard

e__ible   _____   able to be seen

s__n__ible   _____   able to bend

Complete the sentences below. Use the words above.

1. The house on the island is only _____ by boat.
2. His bright red shirt was _____ in the crowd.
3. She called out, but her voice was not _____.
4. Rubber is a _____ material.
5. I believe it is _____ to find a cure for the disease.
6. The most responsible and _____ person will get chosen.
7. He had a _____ accident on holiday.
8. The mushrooms were poisonous. They were not _____.

Now write 5 sentences with the words: gullible, legible, responsible, feasible and incredible.

Book 2: Suffixes 'able' and 'ible'

The suffixes 'able' and 'ible' come from Latin. They mean 'able to be' or 'fit for'. These suffixes change a **verb** like 'adore' into an **adjective** like 'adorable'. For example: 'That puppy is adorable.'

These suffixes sound the same, so how do you know when to spell a word with 'able' or 'ible'?
Firstly, the suffix 'able' is much more common than the suffix 'ible' so it is the more likely spelling. Secondly, if the suffix is added to a base word that is a real word in English, you add the suffix 'able': comfort + able = comfort<u>able</u>.

If the suffix is added to a base word that is not a real word in English, it is usually (but not always) spelled with the suffix 'ible': horr + ible = horr<u>ible</u>.

Break the word up into base word and suffix. Then explain the meaning.

word	base word	suffix	word meaning
readable	read	able	can be read
affordable			
possible			
breakable			
fashionable			
agreeable			
audible			
approachable			
edible			

Can you add suffixes 'able' or 'ible' to these words?

terr_____	remark_____	bear_____	speak_____
horr_____	reason_____	predict_____	adapt_____
incred_____	suit_____	accept_____	vis_____

Book 2: Suffixes 'able' and 'ible'

Go figure!

Can you figure out the meaning of these words? Cut out the boxes in the right column and match them to the boxes in the left column so that they make sense.

This shirt is <u>reversible</u>.	trip was cancelled.
You can't play football here.	It's <u>divisible</u> only by itself and 1.
I like John a lot.	You can wear it inside out too.
It is <u>regrettable</u> that the school	It is <u>valuable</u>.
The summer was very hot.	I am very <u>gullible</u>.
Number 7 is a prime number.	It is not <u>permissible</u>.
That ring belonged to my grandma.	In the shade it was just <u>bearable</u>.
The puppy jumped up and down.	He is very <u>agreeable</u>.
I believe almost anything I am told.	He was very <u>excitable</u>.

Book 2: 4-in-a-row – suffixes 'able' and 'ible'

poss**ible**	bear**able**	agree**able**	convert**ible**	divis**ible**
avail**able**	horr**ible**	advis**able**	valu**able**	gull**ible**
reli**able**	comfort**able**	reason**able**	cap**able**	terr**ible**
suit**able**	lov**able**	incred**ible**	believ**able**	excit**able**
imposs**ible**	inevit**able**	regrett**able**	accept**able**	manage**able**
forgett**able**	excus**able**	flex**ible**	sens**ible**	leg**ible**

Play with two sets of colored counters. Two players take turns to read the word and put a counter on the word. The winner is the first to get four of his/her counters in a row. The winner places a counter on the trophy cup above. The game is played four times until all the trophy cups are covered. Discuss new words with the student to help develop his/her vocabulary.

Additional activities: a) Ask the student to highlight the stress in the word so that he/she can learn to pronounce it correctly. b) Ask the student to split the words up into syllables.

Book 2: Revision 1: base word and suffixes

Underline or highlight the base words. Then write the morphemes in the correct columns. Note that some words may have two suffixes, e.g. help–less–ly.

<u>help</u> less ly   freshness   affordable   usefulness

carefully   ownership   creamy   rested   foolishness

joylessness   leadership   selfishly   cheapest

harmfully   meaningless   frightening

	base word	suffix	suffix
1	help	less	ly
2			
3			
4			
5			
6			
7			
8			
9			
10			
11			
12			
13			
14			
15			
16			

Book 2: Revision 2: adding suffixes

Add the suffixes to the base words below. Remember the spelling tips you have learned.

	base word	add suffix	spelling		base word	add suffix	spelling
1	game	s	games	16	happy	ness	
2	hutch	s		17	beauty	ful	
3	try	ed		18	creepy	ness	
4	beg	ed		19	big	er	
5	grate	ed		20	heavy	er	
6	rally	ed		21	hot	est	
7	race	ing		22	weak	est	
8	nag	ing		23	careful	ly	
9	bully	ing		24	noisy	ly	
10	body	s		25	normal	ly	
11	ploy	s		26	shrunk	en	
12	fry	ing		27	shave	en	
13	use	ful		28	girl	ish	
14	end	less		29	regret	able	
15	penny	less		30	poss	ible	

Correct your errors here:

_____

_____

Book 3: 'Into the Unknown'

Contents

Book 3: prefix – base word – suffix

Morphemes are parts of the word that give it meaning. The **base word** is the main part. The **prefix** is added to the beginning of the word. A **suffix** is added to the end. Prefixes and suffixes can change the meaning of the word. Learning to identify the parts of the words can help you to understand the word and spell it accurately.

Underline the base words. Then write the morphemes in the correct columns.

un **limit** ed   refreshing   holding   replace   reuse

unlikely   reminded   unselfish   impossible

discovered   exported   inaccessible   hopeful

prefix	base word	suffix
un	limit	ed

Book 3: Prefix 'un'

The prefix 'un' comes from Old English and means 'not'. For example, '**un**likely' means 'not likely'. 'Un' also means to 'undo'. For example, to '**un**pack' a bag means to undo the bag that has been packed.

Spelling tip: When the base word begins with the letter 'n', you must keep the prefix: u<u>nn</u>atural, u<u>nn</u>ecessary.

Can you complete these phrases?

an unhappy _____

an unfriendly _____

unacceptable _____

an untrainable _____

an unexpected _____

unlimited _____

an unforgettable _____

an unemployed _____

an unlucky _____

an unnecessary _____

Now complete the diagram below.

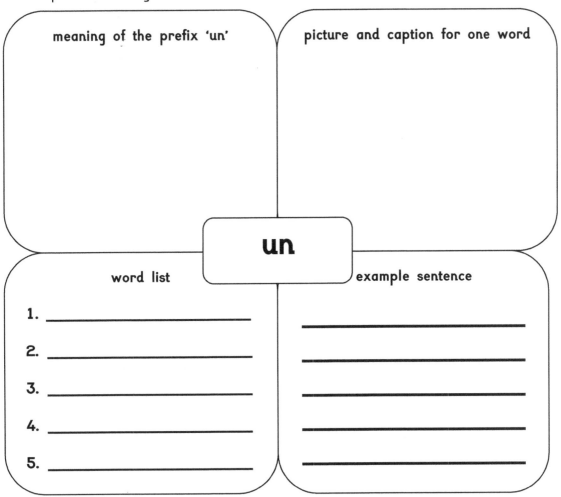

meaning of the prefix 'un'	picture and caption for one word

un

word list	example sentence
1. _____	_____
2. _____	_____
3. _____	_____
4. _____	_____
5. _____	_____

58

Book 3: Prefix 'un' – sentence matching

Go figure!

Can you figure out the meaning of these sentences? Cut out the boxes in the right column and match them to the boxes in the left column so that the sentences make sense.

It will rain on Sunday so it is	It was **uninteresting**.
A seal was spotted in the river.	She **untied** the laces.
The museum visit was disappointing.	a white rabbit hopped out.
Her boots were too tight.	**unlikely** the festival will go ahead.
As the author had died,	This is a very **unusual** sight.
The digger dug up an old Roman	the boy was **unafraid** to speak out.
The magician **unzipped** the bag and	but the manager was **unresponsive**.
Despite all the threats and bullying,	the book remained **unpublished**.
I wrote and complained many times,	villa. It **uncovered** a mosaic floor.

Book 3: Prefix 'un' – word tree

Write the new words you have learned with the prefix 'un' in the word tree.

un = not

un = undo

Can you write a sentence for each of these words?

Book 3: Prefix 'in'

The prefix 'in' comes from Latin and means 'not'. For example, 'incorrect' means 'not correct'. Here are some words with the prefix 'in': **in**complete, **in**visible, **in**elegant, **in**decisive, **in**direct.

Draw a line from the words to their correct meanings.

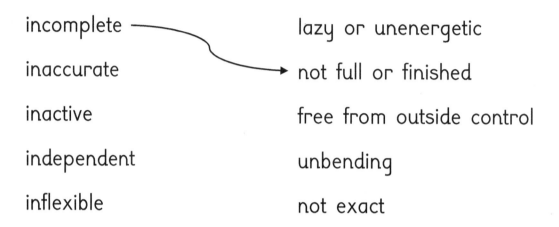

incomplete — — — → lazy or unenergetic

inaccurate   not full or finished

inactive   free from outside control

independent   unbending

inflexible   not exact

Now complete the diagram below.

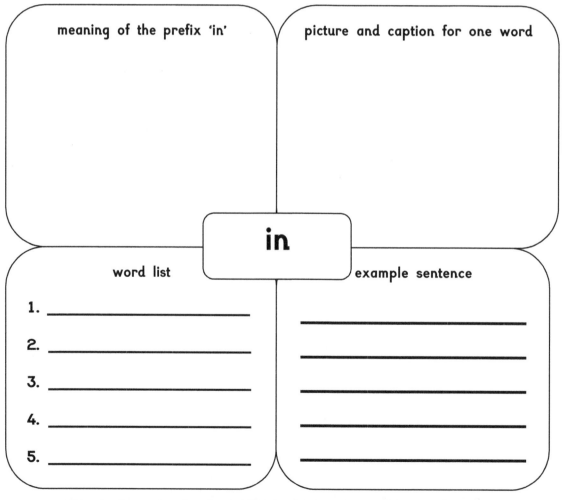

meaning of the prefix 'in'	picture and caption for one word

in

word list	example sentence
1. _____	_____
2. _____	_____
3. _____	_____
4. _____	_____
5. _____	_____

Book 3: Prefix 'in' – sentence matching

Go figure!

Can you figure out the meaning of these sentences? Cut out the boxes in the right column and match them to the boxes in the left column so that the sentences make sense.

The band played too loudly.	didn't mean it. She was **insincere**.
The party was on the beach.	you will be **inconsiderate**.
She apologized, but I knew she	He was **infirm**.
If you don't turn the music down,	treated unfairly.
When I finish school, I will leave	on the horse, but I felt **insecure**.
The old man was very weak.	We were told to dress **informally**.
After falling off, I got straight back	may be **infinite**.
The universe and galaxies	The singer was **inaudible**.
Injustice is when people are	home and live **independently**.

Book 3: Prefix 'in' – word tree

Write the new words you have learned with the prefix 'in' in the word tree.

in = not

Can you write a sentence for each of these words?

Book 3: Prefix 'im'

The prefix 'im' is like the prefix 'in', but it appears before base words that begin with the letters 'm', 'b', and 'p'. It means 'not' or 'the opposite of'. For example: '**im**possible' means 'not possible'.
Spelling tip: When the base word begins with the letter 'm', keep the prefix complete: i**mm**ature.

Draw a line from the words to their correct meanings.

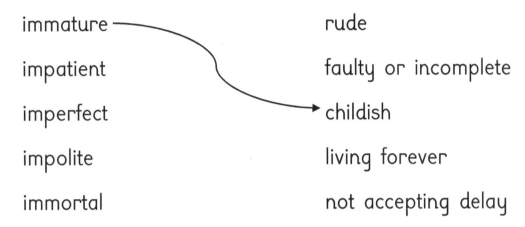

immature   rude

impatient   faulty or incomplete

imperfect   childish

impolite   living forever

immortal   not accepting delay

Now complete the diagram below.

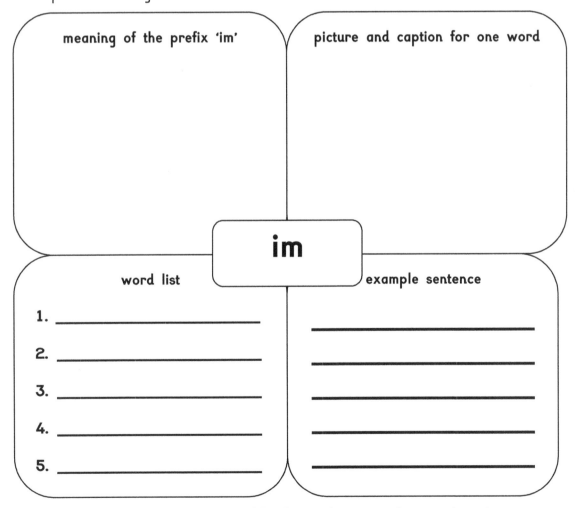

| meaning of the prefix 'im' | picture and caption for one word |

im

| word list | example sentence |

1. _____
2. _____
3. _____
4. _____
5. _____

Book 3: Prefix 'im' – word tree

Write the new words you have learned with the prefix 'im' in the word tree.

im = not

(prefix before base words that begin with the letters 'b', 'm' and 'p')

Can you write a sentence for each of these words?

Book 3: Prefixes 'in' or 'im'?

The prefixes 'in' and 'im' mean the same: 'not'.

Spelling tips:

1. The prefix 'im' comes before base words that begin with the letters 'b', 'm' and 'p'. For example: im**b**alance, im**m**ature, im**p**olite.
2. Always keep the prefix complete, even if the base word starts with the letters 'n' and 'm'. For example: **in**numerate (not numerate) and **im**mature (not mature).

Underline the first letter in the base word. Which prefix should you add?

base word	+ in or + im?	word	word meaning (can you find a synonym?)
patient	im	impatient	short-tempered
possible			
correct			
credible			
secure			
perfect			
mobile			
sincere			
visible			
mortal			
pure			
sane			
valid			
polite			

Book 3: Prefix 'il'

The prefix 'il' is like the prefix 'in', but it appears before base words that begin with the letter 'l'. It means 'not' or 'the opposite of'. For example, 'illegal' means 'not legal'.

Spelling tip: Remember to keep the prefix complete.

Draw a line from the words to their correct meanings.

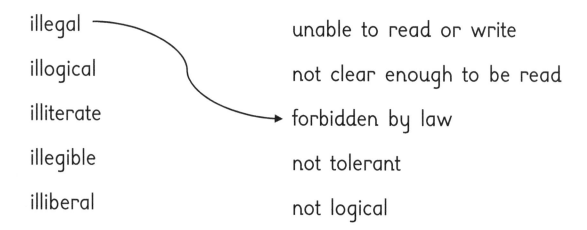

illegal   unable to read or write

illogical   not clear enough to be read

illiterate   forbidden by law

illegible   not tolerant

illiberal   not logical

Now complete the diagram below.

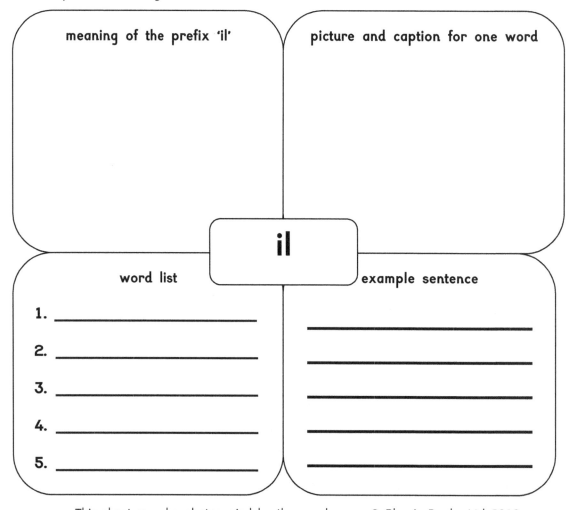

meaning of the prefix 'il'

picture and caption for one word

il

word list

1. _____

2. _____

3. _____

4. _____

5. _____

example sentence

_____

_____

_____

_____

_____

Book 3: Prefix 'il' – word tree

Write the new words you have learned with the prefix 'il' in the word tree.

il = not

(prefix before base words that begin with the letter 'l')

Can you write a sentence for each of these words?

Book 3: Prefix 'ir'

The prefix 'ir' is like the prefix 'in', but it appears before base words that begin with the letter 'r'. It means 'not' or 'the opposite of'. For example, **'irregular'** means 'not regular'.

Spelling tip: Remember to keep the prefix complete, as in the word **'irreligious'**.

Draw a line from the words to their correct meanings.

irresistible   impossible to replace

irreplaceable   too attractive to be resisted

irrational   not connected to anything

irresponsible   not logical or reasonable

irrelevant   not responsible

Now complete the diagram below.

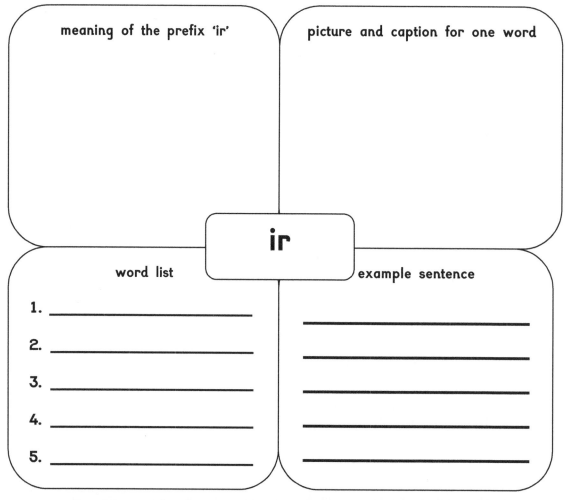

Book 3: Prefix 'ir' – word tree

Write the new words you have learned with the prefix 'ir' in the word tree.

ir = not

(prefix before base words that
begin with the letter 'r')

Can you write a sentence for each of these words?

Book 3: 4-in-a-row – prefixes 'un', 'in', 'im', 'ir' and 'il'

unable	**im**patient	**un**kind	**in**direct	**ir**regular
imprecise	**un**decided	**im**perfect	**il**logical	**in**visible
independent	**il**legal	**un**reliable	**in**conclusive	**il**legible
irrational	**im**moral	**in**credible	**un**expected	**un**healthy
incomplete	**ir**relevant	**il**literate	**im**possible	**un**tangle
infinite	**im**mature	**un**common	**ir**reversible	**un**afraid

Play with two sets of colored counters. Two players take turns to read the word and put a counter on the word. The winner is the first to get four of his/her counters in a row. The winner places a counter on the trophy cup above. The game is played four times until all the trophy cups are covered. Discuss new words with the student to help develop his/her vocabulary.

<u>Additional activities</u>: a) Ask the student to highlight the stress in the word so that he/she can learn to pronounce it correctly. b) Ask the student to split the words up into syllables.

Book 3: Prefixes 'in', 'im', 'il' and 'ir'

The prefixes 'in', 'im', 'il' and 'ir' all mean the same: 'not' or 'the opposite of'.
Spelling tips:
1. 'im' comes before base words that begin with the letters 'b', 'm' and 'p'.
2. 'ir' comes before base words that begin with the letter 'r'.
3. 'il' comes before base words that begin with the letter 'l'.

Remember: Always keep the prefix complete: **im**moral, **ir**regular, **il**legal.

Underline the first letter in the base word. Which prefix should you add?

base word	'in', 'im', 'il' or 'ir'?	word	meaning (can you find a synonym?)
mortal	im	immortal	lives forever
complete			
possible			Can't be done
flexible			
religious			secular
considerate			
logical			
mobile			
responsible			
visible			
polite			
pure			
reversible			
legible			
partial			
active			

Book 3: Prefixes 'un', 'in', 'im', 'il' and 'ir'

Is it '**un**', '**in**', '**im**', '**il**' or '**ir**'? Insert the correct prefix before the base words.

Finn ____folded the map. He was ____patient to get to the next monument. An icy wind began to blow as they reached the snow-capped mountains. Monk was ____able to get warm. He tucked himself snugly inside Finn's tunic. Snow started to fall heavily. The way ahead was almost ____visible. The setting sun cast long shadows across the snow. Monk was shivering. Finn felt it was ____responsible to stay out in the bitter cold. "We need to find a place to camp for the night," he told Kit. "There's a cave on the other side of that bridge," he added. The old wooden bridge was ____secure. Cracked and broken planks made it almost ____possible to find a safe route across. They followed Monk as he clambered ____afraid to cross the ruined bridge. Suddenly, an ____expected mass of tiny screeching bodies flew at their faces. They were a swarm of bats! Finn had an ____rational fear of bats. It was an ____logical fear. He almost fell into the gorge below. As he hung from the bridge, he looked down at the ____measurably dark abyss. ____frightened, Izzy quickly reached out to grab him. Beating away the last of the bats, they clambered up the bank at the end of the bridge. Suddenly, there was an ____credible rumbling sound. They whirled around to see the bridge collapsing behind them. A silent tidal wave of snow slid down the mountain towards them. "Run, or we will end up in that gorge!" yelled Finn.

Book 3: Prefix 'mis'

The prefix **'mis'** comes from Latin. It means 'wrong' or 'wrongly'.
For example: 'mistreat' means 'treat wrongly'.

Spelling tip: Remember to keep the prefix complete, as in the word **'mis**spell'.

Draw a line from the words to their correct meanings.

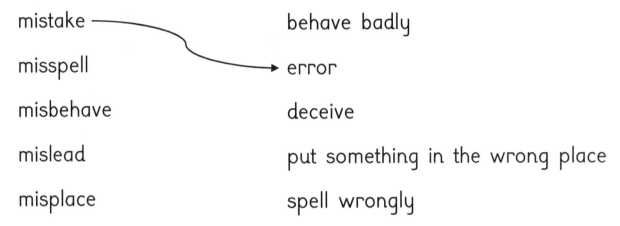

mistake — behave badly

misspell — error

misbehave — deceive

mislead — put something in the wrong place

misplace — spell wrongly

Now complete the diagram below.

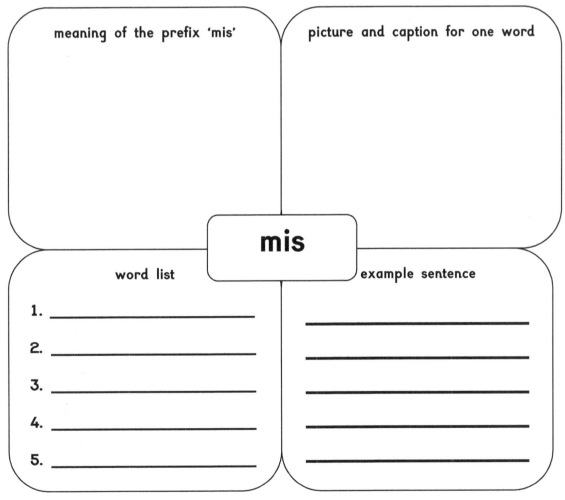

meaning of the prefix 'mis'

picture and caption for one word

mis

word list

1. _____
2. _____
3. _____
4. _____
5. _____

example sentence

_____
_____
_____
_____
_____

Book 3: Prefix 'mis' – sentence matching

Go figure!

Can you figure out the meaning of these sentences? Cut out the boxes in the right column and match them to the boxes in the left column so that the sentences make sense.

He tried to jump over the pond, but	but they were on his head.
I **miscounted** the number of guests.	It was sent to the wrong address.
Grandad **mislaid** his glasses,	**misjudged** the distance and fell in.
Humans should be kind to animals.	There weren't enough cupcakes.
The children laughed when the	losing both his parents.
The criminal told lies to the police.	They should not **mistreat** them.
The boy had the **misfortune** of	**mismanaged** his inheritance.
The man lost all his money. He	teacher **mispronounced** my name.
The parcel was **misdirected.**	He was trying to **mislead** them.

Book 3: Prefix 'mis' – word tree

Write the new words you have learned with the prefix 'mis' in the word tree.

mis = wrong

Can you write a sentence for each of these words?

Book 3: Prefix 'dis'

The prefix 'dis' comes from Latin. It means 'not' and 'undo'.
For example: 'disloyal' means 'not loyal'. It can also mean 'apart', as in the word 'disconnect'.

Spelling tip: Remember to keep the prefix complete, as in the word '**dis**satisfied'.

Draw a line from the words to their correct meanings.

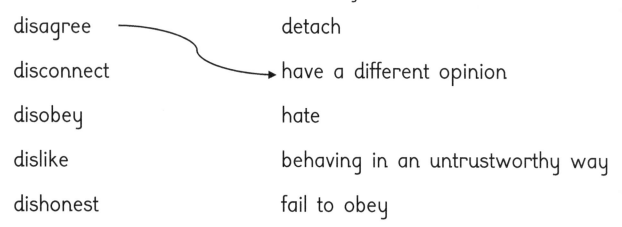

disagree	detach
disconnect	have a different opinion
disobey	hate
dislike	behaving in an untrustworthy way
dishonest	fail to obey

Now complete the diagram below.

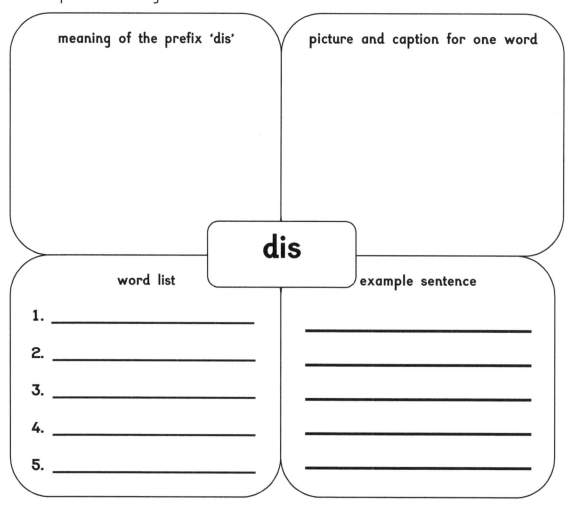

meaning of the prefix 'dis'

picture and caption for one word

dis

word list

1. _____

2. _____

3. _____

4. _____

5. _____

example sentence

_____

_____

_____

_____

_____

Book 3: Prefix 'dis' – sentence matching

Go figure!

Can you figure out the meaning of these sentences? Cut out the boxes in the right column and match them to the boxes in the left column so that the sentences make sense.

When I fell off my horse,	**disqualified** from the race.
The man **disliked** crowds, so he	you will be punished.
It is important not to **disrespect**	appear and then **disappear**.
The patient caught an infection,	about the storm and he capsized.
The runner cheated and was	I **dislocated** my shoulder.
If you **disobey** the school rules,	customer was **dissatisfied**.
The magician made the rabbit	other people.
The package was damaged, so the	so the hospital was **disinfected**.
The sailor **disregarded** the warning	avoided going to crowded places.

Book 3: Prefix 'dis' – word tree

Write the new words you have learned with the prefix 'dis' in the word tree.

dis = not, undo, apart

Can you write a sentence for each of these words?

Book 3: 4-in-a-row – prefixes 'mis' and 'dis'

mistake	**dis**appear	**mis**behave	**dis**tasteful	**mis**lay
misspelled	**mis**treat	**dis**agree	**dis**like	**mis**lead
disconnect	**dis**regard	**mis**read	**mis**use	**dis**honest
misplace	**dis**trust	**mis**judge	**dis**loyal	**dis**satisfied
misprint	**mis**quote	**dis**obey	**dis**order	**dis**own
mismatch	**dis**grace	**mis**fortune	**dis**appoint	**dis**cover

Play with two sets of colored counters. Two players take turns to read the word and put a counter on the word. The winner is the first to get four of his/her counters in a row. The winner places a counter on the trophy cup above. The game is played four times until all the trophy cups are covered. Discuss new words with the student to help develop his/her vocabulary.

Additional activities: a) Ask the student to highlight the stress in the word so that he/she can learn to pronounce it correctly. b) Ask the student to split the words up into syllables.

Book 3: Prefixes 'mis' and 'dis'

Insert these words into the text. Then reread the text to make sure it makes sense.

disbelief – refusal to believe

disheartened – without hope

disorientated – felt confused, a loss of direction

misadventure – an unfortunate incident, a mishap

dislodged – knocked out of position

discover – reveal

The avalanche _____ the snow and it came crashing down the mountainside. The three friends raced to the safety of the cave. It was dark inside the cave and almost impossible to see. Which way should they go? Kit felt _____ in the dark. He lit a torch. The cavern filled with flickering light.

"This is the Kontag gold mine!" said Izzy in _____. "Rumor has it that a creature, known as a viperator, emerged from the depths to take possession of it." She looked around. She looked _____. The viperator was deadly! Would they leave this case alive?

"The orb is glowing," her voice trembled as she pulled it from her pocket. "I think we will _____ the next monument nearby." They scrambled through a series of narrow tunnels. Finally, they arrived at a rocky ledge.

"There's a faint amber glow down there. That must be a good sign!" said Kit.

"A good sign, or a sign we are about to meet that 'viperator!" Izzy replied uncertainly. Would this adventure turn into a _____?

Book 3: Revision 1: prefix – base/root word – suffix

Underline or highlight the base/root words. Then write the morphemes in the correct columns. For example: ir–resist–ible.

	ir <u>resist</u> ible incorrectly unaffordable misbehaving
	dishonestly misspelled impossible invisible disobeyed
	illegally irreversible impatiently illegible
	misprinted disappeared unselfish

	prefix	base/root word	suffix
1	ir	resist	ible
2			
3			
4			
5			
6			
7			
8			
9			
10			
11			
12			
13			
14			
15			
16			

Book 3: Revision 2: adding prefixes

Add the correct prefixes to the base words below.

Is it 'un', 'in', 'im', 'il', 'ir', 'mis' or 'dis'?

	add prefix	base word	spelling		add prefix	base word	spelling
1	un	happy	unhappy	16		appear	
2		mortal		17		possible	
3		regular		18		agree	
4		legal		19		complete	
5		connect		20		direct	
6		correct		21		place	
7		perfect		22		honest	
8		flexible		23		helpful	
9		behave		24		button	
10		cover		25		relevant	
11		able		26		legible	
12		fair		27		secure	
13		visible		28		credible	
14		treat		29		obey	
15		spell		30		polite	

Correct your errors here:

_____

_____

Book 4: 'Roots of Corruption'

Contents

Book 4: Prefix 're'

The prefix **'re'** comes from Latin and means 'again' or 'back'.

Here are some example words: **re**play, **re**turn, **re**mind, **re**visit.

Draw a line from the words to their correct meanings.

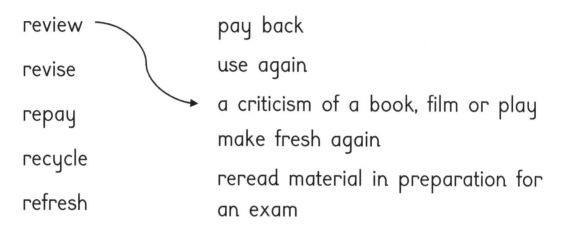

review   pay back

revise   use again

repay   a criticism of a book, film or play

recycle   make fresh again

refresh   reread material in preparation for
                an exam

Now complete the diagram below.

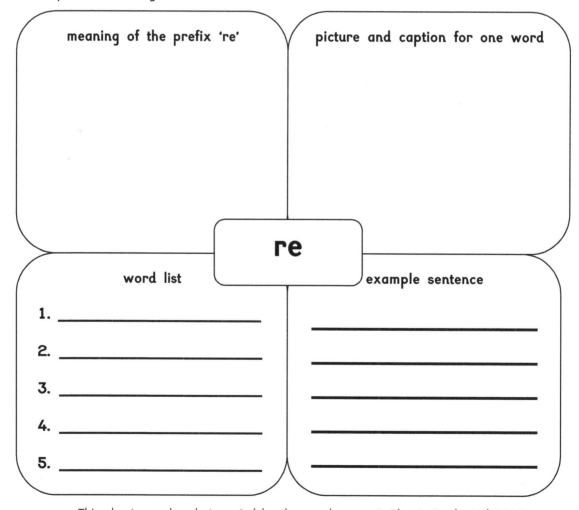

meaning of the prefix 're'

picture and caption for one word

re

word list

1. _____
2. _____
3. _____
4. _____
5. _____

example sentence

_____
_____
_____
_____
_____

Book 4: Prefix 're' – sentence matching

Go figure!

Can you figure out the meaning of these sentences? Cut out the boxes in the right column and match them to the boxes in the left column so that the sentences make sense.

The old man could not **remember**	home, so I had to **reheat** it.
The detective had to	Next year I'll **redouble** my efforts.
The kids loved to watch that video.	I got stung when I **retrieved** it.
The food was cold when I got	he didn't know how to **react**.
The ball landed in the nettles.	where he lived.
This year I didn't win the race.	They **replayed** it again and again.
When I stood up to the bully,	**re-examine** the evidence.
Our school uniform is old-fashioned	it stopped raining.
The tennis match **resumed** after	and needs to be **redesigned**.

This sheet may be photocopied by the purchaser.   © Phonic Books Ltd 2019

Book 4: Prefix 're'

Insert these words into the text. Then reread the text to make sure it makes sense.

rebounded – bounced back in the air   **responded** – answered

recalled – remembered   **revive** – bring back to life, restore

repeated – did again   **regained** – got something back after losin(

reminded – caused a person to remember

Gliding on the back of Ignia was both exciting and terrifying.

"Grab some sleep while you can!" yelled Finn over the racing noise of the wind. Izzy could not sleep. Instead she _____ the amazing adventures they had been through. They _____ her of the exciting adventures she had experienced with her father. At noon they arrived at their next stopping point.

Ignia hovered over a forest, looking for a place to land. She tried to land, but her wings were huge and the trees were swaying violently. Suddenly she began to plummet! Spiked branches clutched at Ignia as if they were trying to drag her from the sky. Ignia broke free and _____ some height, but the long vines grasped at her legs.

Ignia _____ her attempt to land, but she smashed through the trees and crashed to the ground. She _____ back into the air, but the branches clawed at her with strong muscular arms. Ignia careered across the forest floor and came to a halt. Her limp body lay lifeless on the ground.

"Ignia is unconscious! We must _____ her!" Izzy scrambled off Ignia's back. "How can we help her?"

"It's her wing. It's badly twisted," Finn _____ sadly.

Book 4: Prefix 're' – word tree

Write the new words you have learned with the prefix 're' in the word tree.

re = again
re = back

Can you write a sentence for each of these words?

Book 4: Prefix 'pre'

The prefix **'pre'** comes from Latin. It means 'before'.

Here are some example words: **pre**view, **pre**vent, **pre**pay, **pre**fix.

Draw a line from the words to their correct meanings.

preview

to take precautions

prejudice

predict

premature

a bad opinion formed before having knowledge of something

an advance showing of a film or play

tell the future, prophesy

take steps to prevent something bad happening

too early

Now complete the diagram below.

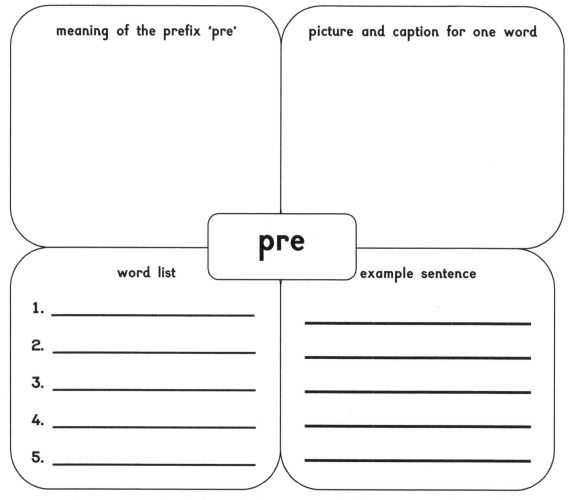

meaning of the prefix 'pre'	picture and caption for one word

pre

word list	example sentence
1. _____	_____
2. _____	_____
3. _____	_____
4. _____	_____
5. _____	_____

Book 4: Prefix 'pre' – sentence matching

Go figure!

Can you figure out the meaning of these sentences? Cut out the boxes in the right column and match them to the boxes in the left column so that the sentences make sense.

I **predicted** that my soccer team	before of the trip.
The **preview** took place in a	**preceded** the disco party.
A **prefix** is the part of the word	would win the match 2:1.
There was a lot to **prepare**	it was available in the shops.
The wedding service	a storm was coming.
I **pre-ordered** the video before	lived in the countryside.
In **preindustrial** times, most people	and **prevented** a disaster.
The firemen put out the fire quickly	small cinema.
We took **precautions** as we knew	that comes before the base word.

Book 4: Prefix 'pre' – word tree

Write the new words you have learned with the prefix 'pre' in the word tree.

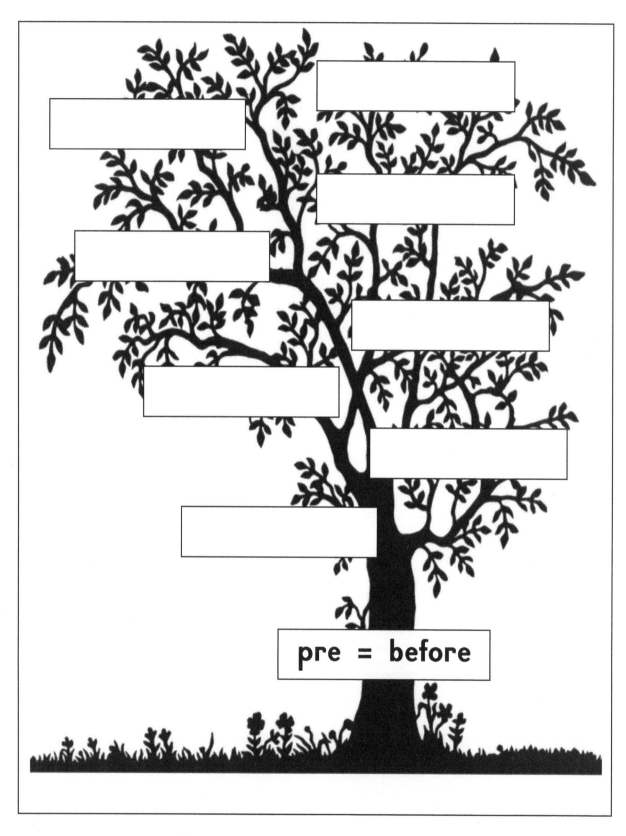

pre = before

Can you write a sentence for each of these words?

Book 4: Prefixes 're' and 'pre'

Insert the prefixes 're' or 'pre' into the text. Then reread the text to make sure it makes sense.

Ignia lay lifeless on the forest floor, her wing badly twisted.

"Look!" said Finn. "The wing is losing its color." The fire colors slowly ____treated from the wing. It was now gray and dull.

"We have to find a way to ____store her!" sobbed Izzy. "There will be herbs in the forest strong enough to do it."

Finn eyed the swaying trees around them. He had a ____monition that something terrible was going to happen in this threatening forest.

"Something bad will happen here," he ____dicted.

The orb began to judder. Izzy turned it around. It ____vealed a glowing symbol of a waterfall.

Finn looked around anxiously. Was the forest closer than before? Was it advancing towards them? "We must find the amber jewel, but we can't leave Ignia unprotected."

Luckily, Kit had ____packed some matches. He quickly built a small campfire as a ____caution. "This will ____vent any unwelcome visitors coming near," he said.

They left the wounded bird beside the fire and set off into the dense forest. They fought their way through the thick undergrowth. Kit scrambled up a tall tree to survey the landmarks. He lost his footing and almost fell. He dangled from a branch. Monk ____acted quickly, scampered up and thrust a branch towards him. Shaken from his fall, he paused and then ____sumed the climb. Finally he reached the top.

"I can see the whole forest from up here!" he yelled in amazement.

Book 4: Prefix 'post'

The prefix **'post'** comes from Latin. It means 'after'.

Here are some example words: **post**pone, **post**graduate, **post**mortem.

Draw a line from the words to their correct meanings.

postmeridian (p.m.)

posthumous

postscript (P.S.)

postmortem

postpone

an additional remark at the end of a letter

afternoon

to arrange for something to take place at a later date

happening after a person's death

an examination of a dead body to find out the cause of death

Now complete the diagram below.

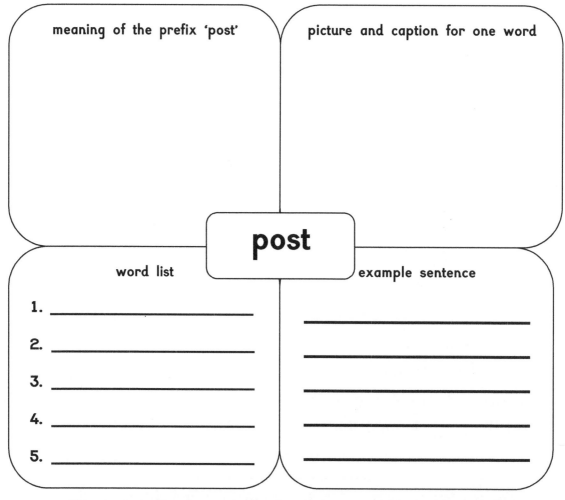

meaning of the prefix 'post'

picture and caption for one word

post

word list

1. _____

2. _____

3. _____

4. _____

5. _____

example sentence

_____

_____

_____

_____

_____

Book 4: Prefix 'post' – sentence matching

Go figure!

Can you figure out the meaning of these sentences? Cut out the boxes in the right column and match them to the boxes in the left column so that the sentences make sense.

I **postponed** the meeting because	that is added to the end of a letter.
Postmeridian (p.m.) means	clues from the **postmortem**.
Some soldiers suffer from	after shooting a film.
A **postscript** (P.S.) is a remark	**posthumously**, after they die.
A **postgraduate** course is for	it snowed heavily.
The detective hoped to get more	after they have given birth.
A **postnatal** clinic is for mothers	a student who has a first degree.
Postproduction takes place	**post-war** stress disorder.
Some artists are only famous	'afternoon' in Latin.

Book 4: Prefix 'post' – word tree

Write the new words you have learned with the prefix 'post' in the word tree.

post = after

Can you write a sentence for each of these words?

Book 4: Prefixes 'ante' and 'anti'

The prefix **'ante'** comes from Latin and means 'before', as in the word **'ante**chamber', which is a small room that leads to a larger room.

This is often confused with the prefix **'anti'** which comes from Greek and means 'against' or 'opposite' as in the word **'anti**social' – the opposite of 'social'.

Words with the prefix 'ante'	Words with the prefix 'anti'
antecede – to come before **antechamber** – a small room leading to a large one **antenatal** – before birth	**antisocial** – not social **antihero** – opposite of hero **anticlockwise** – the opposite direction to how the hands of the clock move

Insert the correct word into the sentences below. Use the words above.

1. The _____ led the explorers to a large room with a tomb.

2. He didn't have friends because his behavior was _____.

3. Dinosaurs _____ mammals by millions of years.

4. The young mothers met at an _____ class.

5. I like books in which the main character is an _____.

6. I had to turn the key _____ to open the door.

Write a sentence for each of these words: antiseptic, antidote, antipathy and antibiotics.

Book 4: Prefix 'ante' – word tree

Write the new words you have learned with the prefix 'ante' in the word tree.

ante = before

Can you write a sentence for each of these words?

Book 4: Prefix 'anti' – word tree

Write the new words you have learned with the prefix 'anti' in the word tree.

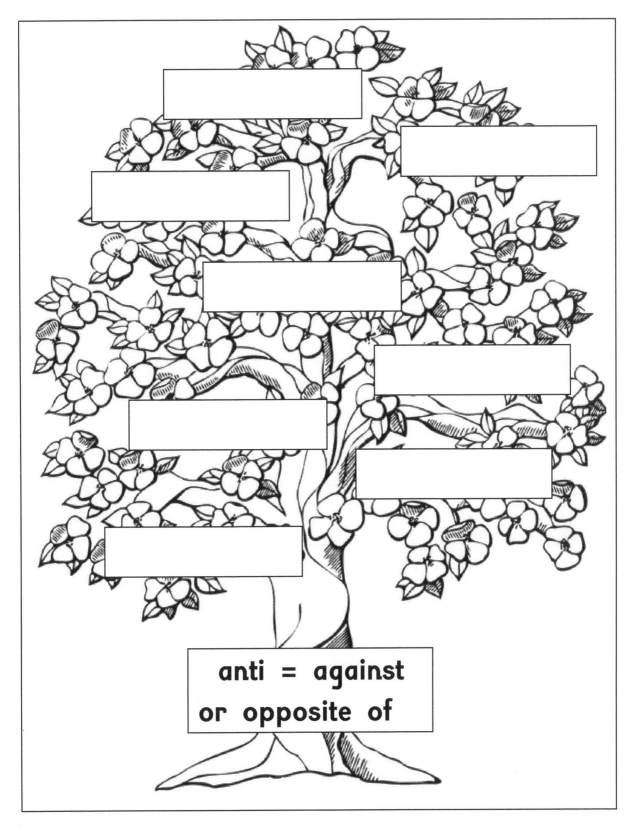

anti = against
or opposite of

Can you write a sentence for each of these words?

Book 4: 4-in-a-row – prefixes 're', 'pre', 'post', 'ante' and 'anti'

rebound	**pre**pare	**re**gain	**post**pone	**re**trieve
antecedent	**anti**biotics	**re**apply	**pre**vent	**re**design
antidote	**re**peat	**re**form	**pre**judice	**anti**septic
antihero	**re**flect	**pre**caution	**post**mortem	**re**vert
predestined	**ante**natal	**post**script	**re**-evalate	**pre**fix
re-examine	**anti**pathy	**ante**date	**re**book	**pre**mix

Play with two sets of colored counters. Two players take turns to read the word and put a counter on the word. The winner is the first to get four of his/her counters in a row. The winner places a counter on the trophy cup above. The game is played four times until all the trophy cups are covered. Discuss new words with the student to help develop his/her vocabulary.

Additional activities: a) Ask the student to highlight the stress in the word so that he/she can learn to pronounce it correctly. b) Ask the student to split the words up into syllables.

Book 4: Revision 1: prefix – base/root word – suffix

Underline or highlight the base/root words. Then write the morphemes in the correct columns. For example: re–fresh–ing.

| | re fresh ing   predicted   revisited   unreliable |
| postpone   antechamber   discovered   prejudge   antihero |
| anticlockwise   antecede   re–enter   previewed |
| impossible   preventing   inescapable |

	prefix	base/root word	suffix
1	re	fresh	ing
2			
3			
4			
5			
6			
7			
8			
9			
10			
11			
12			
13			
14			
15			
16			

Book 4: Revision 2: adding prefixes

Add the correct prefix to the base/root words below.

Is it 're', 'pre', 'post', 'ante' or 'anti'?

	add prefix	base/root word	spelling		add prefix	base/root word	spelling
1	pre	vent	prevent	16		appear	
2		mind		17		fix	
3		meridian	p.m.	18		social	
4		meridian	a.m.	19		judice	
5		vise		20		dote	
6		natal		21		sume	
7		septic		22		pay	
8		member		23		pare	
9		cover		24		consider	
10		dict		25		fresh	
11		chamber		26		order	
12		caution		27		cede	
13		view		28		pone	
14		flect		29		arrange	
15		cycle		30		ject	

Correct your errors here:

_____

_____

Book 5: 'Trials and Trickery'

Contents

Book 5: Prefix 'uni'

The prefix **'uni'** comes from Latin and means 'one'.

For example: **'uni**corn' means 'a horse with one horn'.

Draw a line from the words to the correct definitions.

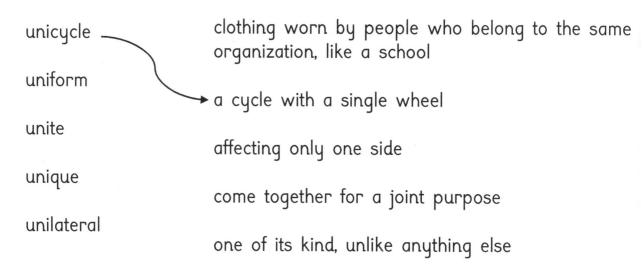

unicycle — clothing worn by people who belong to the same organization, like a school

uniform → a cycle with a single wheel

unite — affecting only one side

unique — come together for a joint purpose

unilateral — one of its kind, unlike anything else

Complete the diagram below.

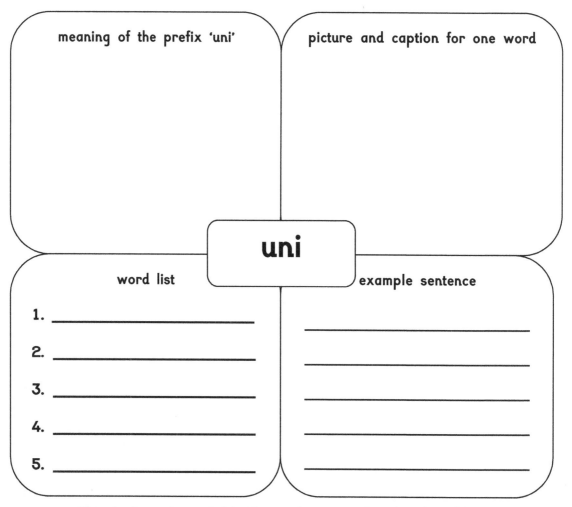

meaning of the prefix 'uni'	picture and caption for one word

uni

word list	example sentence
1. _____	_____
2. _____	_____
3. _____	_____
4. _____	_____
5. _____	_____

Book 5: Prefix 'uni' – sentence matching

Go figure!

Can you figure out the meaning of these sentences? Cut out the boxes in the right column and match them to the boxes in the left column so that they make sense.

My favorite character in the	to ride a **unicycle**.
Panda bears are unique animals	dress the same way.
In circus school, one can learn	millions of galaxies.
School **uniforms** make everyone	high school.
Many workers joined the **union**	fantasy story is the **unicorn**.
The **universe** has millions and	**united** and helped one another.
I may go to a **university** after	to fight together for their rights.
After the disaster, the people	decision to stop fighting the war.
One army made a **unilateral**	and must be saved from extinction.

This sheet may be photocopied by the purchaser.   © Phonic Books Ltd 2019

Book 5: Prefix 'uni' – word tree

Write the new words you have learned with the prefix 'uni' in the word tree.

uni = one

Can you write a sentence for each of these words?

Book 5: Prefix 'bi'

The prefix **'bi'** comes from Latin and means 'two' or 'twice'.

For example: a **bi**cycle is a vehicle with two wheels.

Draw a line from the words to the correct definitions.

bilingual field glasses (with a lens for each eye)

bimonthly speaking two languages fluently

biped occurring every two months or twice a month

bilateral an animal that uses two legs for walking

binoculars affecting two sides

Complete the diagram below.

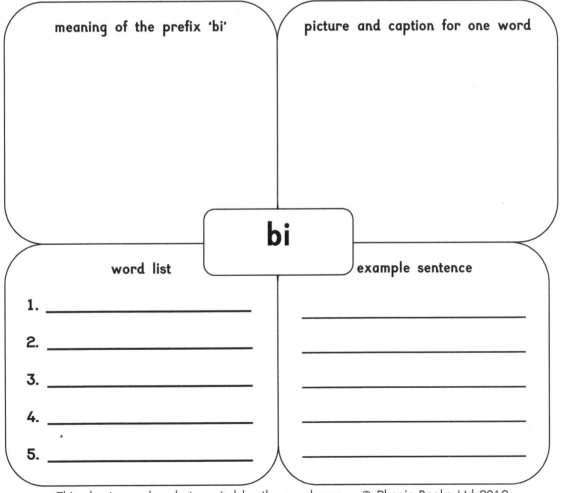

| meaning of the prefix 'bi' | picture and caption for one word |

bi

| word list | example sentence |

1. _____

2. _____

3. _____

4. _____

5. _____

Book 5: Prefix 'bi' – sentence matching

Go figure!

Can you figure out the meaning of these sentences? Cut out the boxes in the right column and match them to the boxes in the left column so that they make sense.

When I ride my **bicycle**, I put	into two halves.
If you are **bilingual**, you can	my helmet on.
Humans walk on two feet, so they	up every two months.
Birdwatchers use **binoculars** to	every two weeks.
The **biweekly** magazine arrives	speak two languages fluently.
A **bimonthly** check-up is a check-	sides are exactly the same.
Twice a year, the family has a	are **bipeds.**
Bilateral symmetry is when two	see the birds close up.
To **bisect** means to cut something	**biannual** holiday.

Book 5: Prefix 'bi' – word tree

Write the new words you have learned with the prefix 'bi' in the word tree.

bi = twice or two

Can you write a sentence for each of these words?

Book 5: Prefix 'tri'

The prefix **'tri'** comes from Latin and Greek and means 'three'.

For example: **'tri**angle' means a shape with three sides and three angles.

Draw a line from the words to the correct definitions.

tricycle

triceratops

trio

trident

trilogy

a herb-eating dinosaur with three horns

a set of three people or things

a vehicle with three wheels – one at the front and two at the back

a group of three related novels, films or plays

a three-pronged spear often depicted with the god Poseidon

Complete the diagram below.

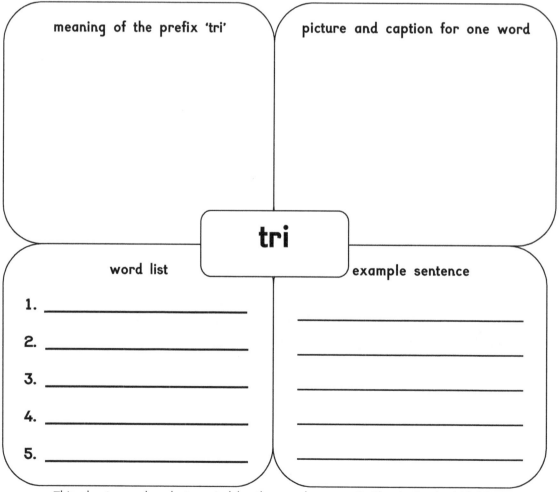

meaning of the prefix 'tri'

picture and caption for one word

tri

word list

1. _____

2. _____

3. _____

4. _____

5. _____

example sentence

_____

_____

_____

_____

_____

Book 5: Prefix 'tri' – sentence matching

Go figure!

Can you figure out the meaning of these sentences? Cut out the boxes in the right column and match them to the boxes in the left column so that the sentences make sense.

The author is writing the third	you get the number 9.
A **triangle** has three sides and	English, French and Spanish.
Young children ride **tricycles**	running, swimming and cycling.
If you **triple** the number 3,	flute and violin.
My dad is **trilingual**. He speaks	book in the **trilogy**.
The Greek god Poseidon is usually	because they can't balance well.
In next year's **triathlon**, I will be	herbivores.
Triceratops were gentle	shown holding a **trident**.
The musical **trio** played the piano,	three angles.

Book 5: Prefix 'tri' – word tree

Write the new words you have learned with the prefix 'tri' in the word tree.

tri = three

Can you write a sentence for each of these words?

Book 5: Prefix 'quad'

The prefix **'quad'** comes from Latin and Greek and means 'four' or 'fourth'.

For example: **quad**rangle is a four-sided shape, such as a rectangle or a square.

Draw a line from the words to the correct definitions.

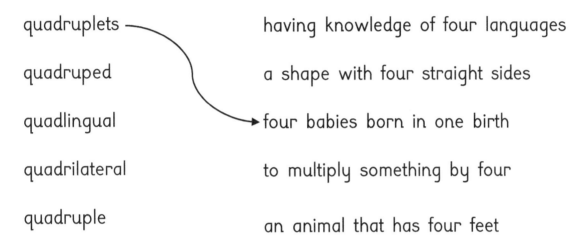

quadruplets — having knowledge of four languages

quadruped — a shape with four straight sides

quadlingual — four babies born in one birth

quadrilateral — to multiply something by four

quadruple — an animal that has four feet

Complete the diagram below.

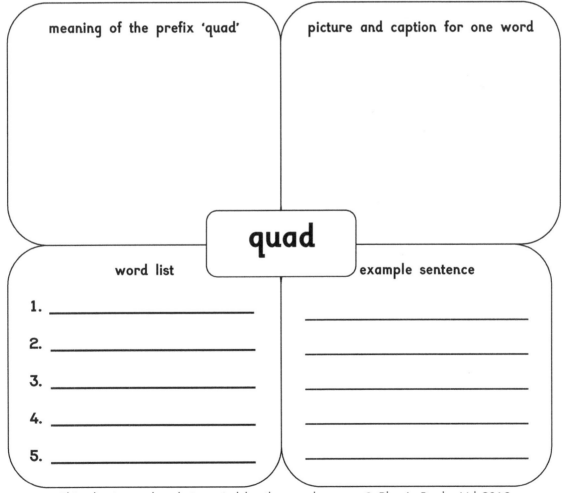

meaning of the prefix 'quad'	picture and caption for one word

quad

word list	example sentence
1. _____	_____
2. _____	_____
3. _____	_____
4. _____	_____
5. _____	_____

Book 5: Prefix 'quad' – sentence matching

Go figure!

Can you figure out the meaning of these sentences? Cut out the boxes in the right column and match them to the boxes in the left column so that they make sense.

A square has four sides and four	**quadrennial** (occur every 4 years).
The mother needed extra help	you get the number 20.
The Olympic Games are	something into four parts.
If you **quadruple** the number 5,	to look after her **quadruplets**.
Many people in Europe speak four	has four **quadrants**.
Horses are **quadrupeds,**	angles, so it is a **quadrangle**.
A circle divided into quarters	four horses is called a **quadriga**.
A Roman chariot drawn by	but humans are bipeds.
To **quadrisect** means to cut	languages. They are **quadlingual**.

Book 5: Prefix 'quad' – word tree

Write the new words you have learned with the prefix 'quad' in the word tree.

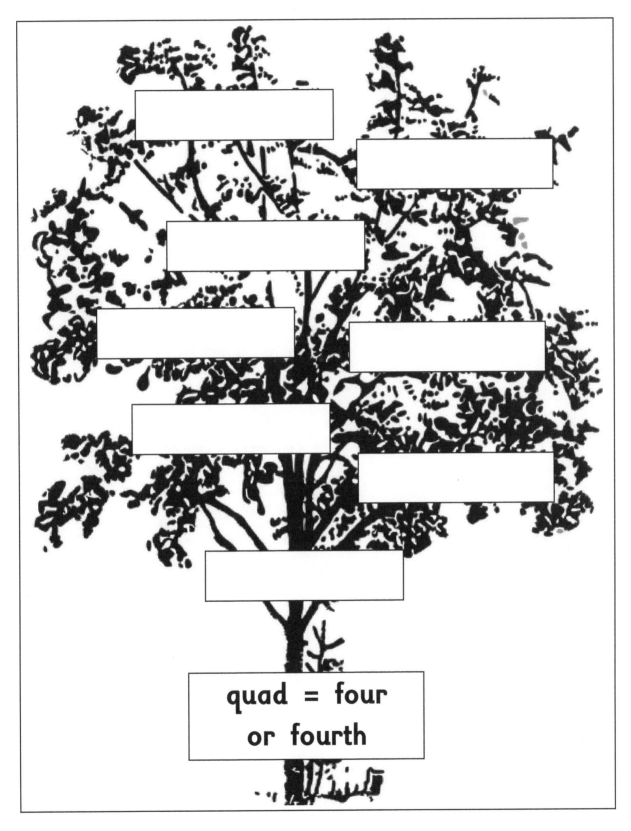

quad = four
or fourth

Can you write a sentence for each of these words?

Book 5: Root word 'dec'/prefixes 'deci';'deca'

The root word **'dec'** is a Latin form of the Greek word 'deka', meaning 'ten', e.g. a **'dec**ade' means 'ten years'. The prefix **'deci'** means 'one-tenth', e.g. a **'deci**liter' is one-tenth of a liter. The prefix **'deca'** means 'having ten', e.g. **'deca**gon' is a shape that has ten sides.

Draw a line from the words to the correct definitions.

December   a system of numbers based on the number ten

decathlon   the tenth month of the Roman calendar

decimate   one tenth of a meter

decimal   to kill or destroy a large proportion

decimeter   an athletic competition in which the competitor participates in ten different events

Complete the diagram below.

meaning of the root word 'dec'
meaning of the prefixes 'deci'/'deca'

picture and caption for one word

dec, deci, deca

word list

1. _____
2. _____
3. _____
4. _____
5. _____

example sentence

_____
_____
_____
_____
_____

 © Phonic Books Ltd 2019

Book 5: Root word 'dec'/prefixes 'deci','deca' sentence matching

Go figure!

Can you figure out the meaning of these sentences? Cut out the boxes in the right column and match them to the boxes in the left column so that they make sense.

I am 25 years old and a **decade**	and is ten centimeters long.
December used to be the 10th	walking legs, like a crab or lobster.
A **decimeter** is a tenth of a meter	how to use **decimals** and fractions.
A **decapod** has five pairs of	ago I was 15.
The hurricane **decimated** most of	includes ten different athletic sports.
In elementary school we learned	sides and ten angles.
Decalogue is another word for the	month in the Roman calendar.
A **decathlon** competition	the trees in the forest.
A **decagon** is a shape with ten	Ten Commandments.

Book 5: Root word 'dec'/prefixes 'deci';'deca' – word tree

Write the new words you have learned with the root word 'dec' and the prefixes 'deci'/'deca' in the word tree.

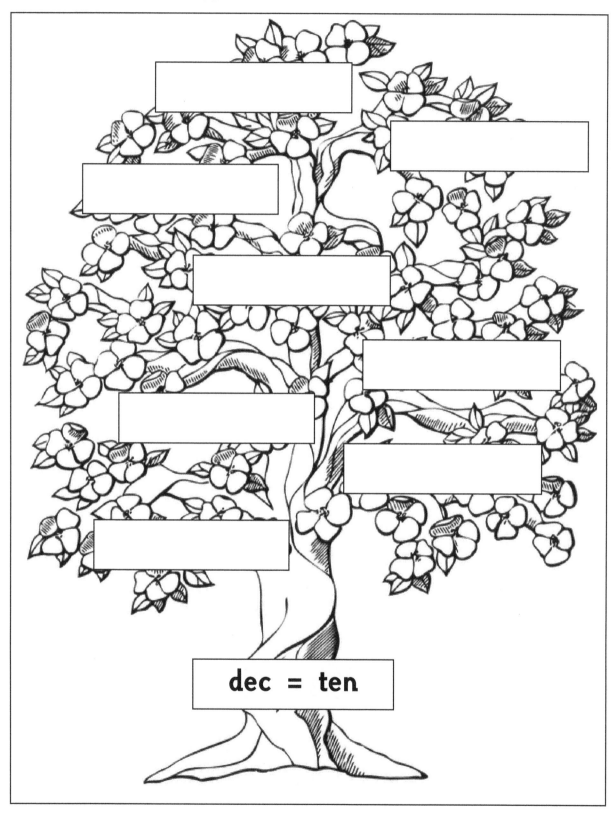

dec = ten

Can you write a sentence for each of these words?

Book 5: Root word 'cent' / prefix 'cent'

The root word **'cent'** comes from Latin and means 'a hundred', e.g. a **'cent**ury' means 'a hundred years'. The prefix **'centi'** means 'one-hundredth', e.g. **'centi**meter' means one-hundredth of a meter.

Draw a line from the words to the correct definitions.

centimeter   one hundredth anniversary of an important event

percent   a measurement of one hundredth of a meter

cent   one hundredth of a dollar

centigrade   a part in every hundred

centenary   the Celsius scale of temperature

Complete the diagram below.

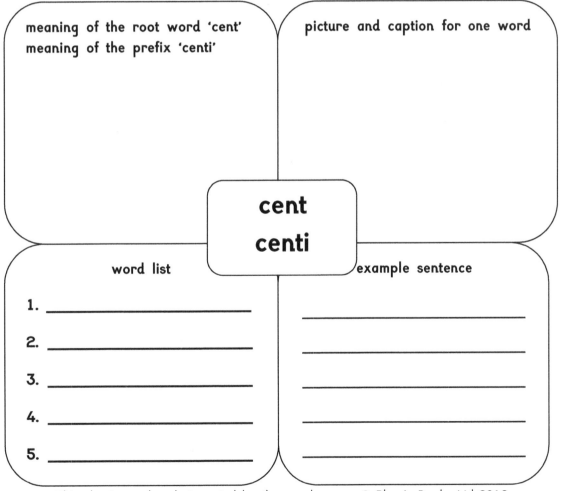

meaning of the root word 'cent'
meaning of the prefix 'centi'

picture and caption for one word

cent
centi

word list

1. _____

2. _____

3. _____

4. _____

5. _____

example sentence

_____

_____

_____

_____

_____

Book 5: Root word 'cent'/prefix 'centi' sentence matching

Go figure!

Can you figure out the meaning of these sentences? Cut out the boxes in the right column and match them to the boxes in the left column so that they make sense.

The industrial revolution began in	**cents**. A dime is ten **cents**.
In the future, many people will	the 18th **century**.
A dollar is one hundred	many legs.
Fifty **percent** is the same as	**centigrade** in the shade today.
A **centipede** is an arthropod with	in the Roman army.
I had to shorten the curtains	live to become **centenarians**.
The temperature was 30 degrees	of the author's death.
There was a **centenary** celebration	by ten **centimeters**.
A **centurion** was a commander	a half of something.

Book 5: Root word 'cent'/prefix 'centi' – word tree

Write the new words you have learned with the root word 'cent' and the prefix 'centi' in the word tree.

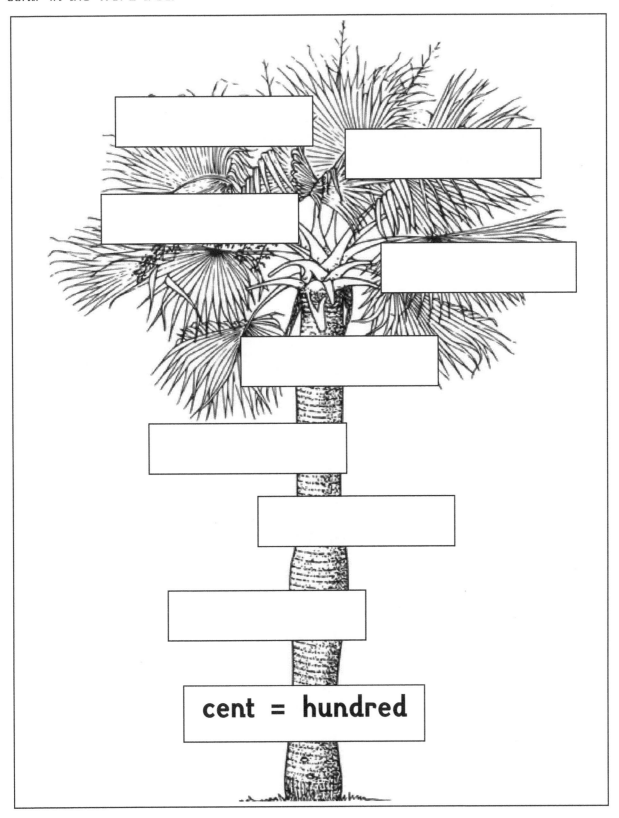

cent = hundred

Can you write a sentence for each of these words?

Book 5: 'uni', 'bi', 'tri', 'quad', 'dec', 'deca', 'cent', 'centi'

Is it 'uni', 'bi', 'tri', 'quad', 'dec', 'deca', 'cent' or 'centi'? Fill in the correct prefixes.

1. A _____angle has three sides and three angles.
2. A _____cycle has two wheels.
3. One hundred years is called a _____ury.
4. A _____ruped walks on four legs.
5. Ten years is called a _____ade.
6. When there is only one of something it is _____que.
7. When students all wear the same clothing in a school, it is called a _____form.
8. When something is mostly destroyed, it is _____imated.
9. When someone speaks three languages, he or she is _____lingual.
10. To multiply a number by four is to _____ruple it.
11. When three babies are born in one birth, they are _____plets.
12. A meter is one hundred _____meters long.
13. A magical creature with one horn is a _____corn.
14. In a _____thlon, the competitor has to compete in ten different events.
15. A _____lateral agreement means an agreement reached by two sides.

Book 5: Prefix 'multi'

The prefix **'multi'** comes from Latin and means 'many'.

For example: **'multi**colored' means 'many colored'.

Draw a line from the words to the correct definitions.

multinational   made up of or relating to people of many races

multitude

                        including or involving a number of countries

multiracial

                        increase a number by multiplication

multiply

                        a large number of people or things

multimillionaire

                        a person who possesses many millions of dollars

Complete the diagram below.

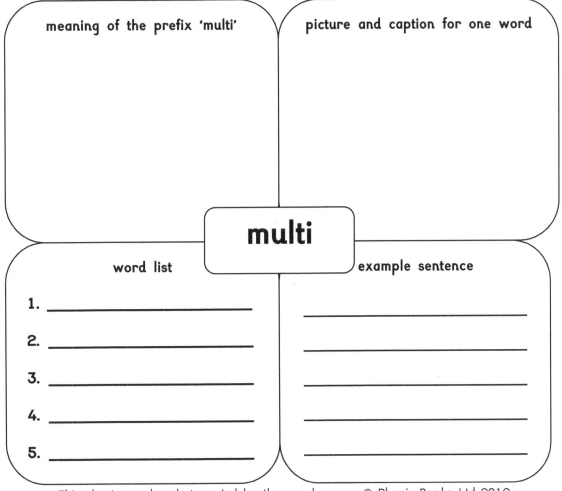

meaning of the prefix 'multi'	picture and caption for one word

multi

word list	example sentence
1. _____	_____
2. _____	_____
3. _____	_____
4. _____	_____
5. _____	_____

Book 5: Prefix 'multi' – sentence matching

Go figure!

Can you figure out the meaning of these sentences? Cut out the boxes in the right colum
and match them to the boxes in the left column so that the sentences make sense.

A **multitude** of people came to	it has seven colors.
If you **multiply** the number 3 by	with more than one syllable.
The children learned to sing their	the demonstration.
A rainbow is **multicolored** because	delicious **multi-ethnic** foods.
The United Nations is a	**multiplication** tables.
A **multisyllabic** word is a word	painting, sculpture and video art.
In Europe many people grow up	**multinational** organization.
The **multimedia** exhibition included	**multilingual**.
At the food festival we tasted	5, you get 15.

Book 5: Prefix 'multi' – word tree

Write the new words you have learned with the prefix 'multi' in the word tree.

multi = many

Can you write a sentence for each of these words?

Book 5: 'uni', 'bi', 'tri', 'quad', 'dec', 'cent', 'multi'

Insert these words into the text. Then reread the text to make sure it makes sense.

combined   trio   century   united

multiple   centimeter   multicolored

The (three) _____ clambered across the stones on all fours. Monk rode on Finn's back, pointing at the (many colored) _____ letters. They were afraid of stepping on the wrong stone and plummeting into the misty depths beneath them. Soon they arrived at the bottom of a flight of golden steps. They could hear the golem roaring with fury behind them. Finn glanced back with dread.

At the top of the stairs was an ancient tree. It looked as if it had been there for at least a (hundred years) _____. A riddle was written on the tree. "I am tall when I am young and short when I am old." Izzy read it out loud. She knew that if they (joined together) _____ their thinking powers they would figure it out.

Kit studied the strange images carved into the tree. "I've got it! It's a candle! A candle melts and gets smaller over time as it burns!" he yelled. Now the golem was clambering up the steps. His body was clumsily formed of (many) _____ broken rocks that were glued together. He was just (one hundredth of a meter) _____s away from the top of the steps. They had to keep the golem out in the rain! The three friends held hands at the top of the steps. They stood bravely, (together as one) _____ against the golem.

Book 5: 4-in-a-row – 'uni', 'bi', 'tri', 'quad', 'dec', 'cent', 'multi'

uniform	**bi**cycle	**tri**angle	**quad**ruped	**cent**ury
multitude	**tri**lingual	**Dec**ember	**multi**–ethnic	**uni**corn
bilateral	**quad**rant	**cent**igrade	**cent**imeter	per**cent**
unisex	**bi**annual	**quad**rangle	**cent**enarian	**multi**ple
decimate	**quad**ruple	**tri**ple	**bi**lingual	**uni**verse
biweekly	**quad**ruplets	**tri**plets	**cent**	**dec**ade

Play with two sets of colored counters. Two players take turns to read the word and put a counter on the word. The winner is the first to get four of his/her counters in a row. The winner places a counter on the trophy cup above. The game is played four times until all the trophy cups are covered. Discuss new words with the student to help develop his/her vocabulary.

Additional activities: a) Ask the student to highlight the stress in the word so that he/she can learn to pronounce it correctly. b) Ask the student to split the words up into syllables.

Book 5: Revision 1 – prefix – base/root word – suffix

Underline or highlight the base/root words. Then write the morphemes in the correct columns. For example: multi-<u>color</u>-ed

multi <u>color</u> ed	unaffordable	triangle	disregarded
percentage	antechamber	re-entered	prevented
anticlockwise	bicycle	decade	misspelled
inaccessible	uniformed	multiply	universe

	prefix	base/root word	suffix
1	multi	color	ed
2			
3			
4			
5			
6			
7			
8			
9			
10			
11			
12			
13			
14			
15			
16			

Book 5: Revision 2: adding prefixes

Add the correct prefixes to the morphemes below. Is it 'uni', 'bi', 'tri', 'quad', 'deci', 'deca', 'centi' or 'multi'? (In some instances you can use more than one prefix.)

	add prefix		spelling		add prefix		spelling
1		form		16		pede	
2		cycle		17		pod	
3		angle		18		plets	
4		liter		19		rant	
5		mal		20		ceratops	
6		corn		21		tude	
7		lingual		22		racial	
8		national		23		versity	
9		ple		24		on	
10		verse		25		fy	
11		lateral		26		noculars	
12		ple		27		sect	
13		ply		28		mate	
14		meter		29		ceps	
15		grade		30		athlon	

Correct your errors here:

_____

_____

This sheet may be photocopied by the purchaser. © Phonic Books Ltd 2019

Book 6: 'Impossible Transformation'

Contents

Book 6: Prefix 'sub'

> The prefix **'sub'** comes from Latin and means 'under' or 'from below'.
>
> For example: a **sub**marine is a warship that navigates under the sea.

Draw a line from the words to the correct definitions.

submerge   existing or occurring under the earth's surface

subtract   cause something to be under water

submissive   take away

subterranean   obedient and passive

subcontinent   part of a larger continent that covers a land mass

Complete the diagram below.

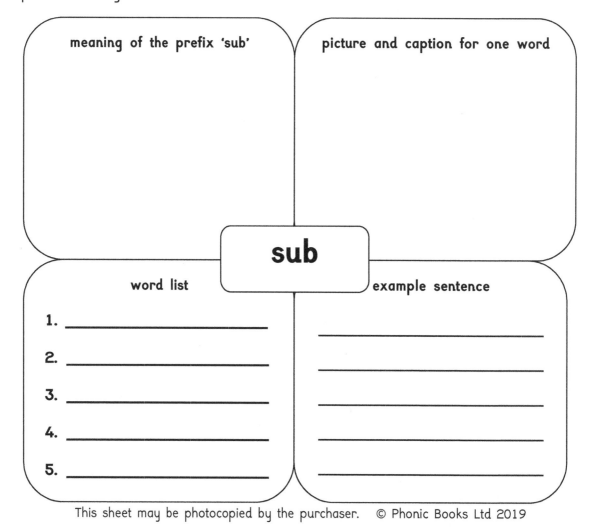

meaning of the prefix 'sub'	picture and caption for one word

sub

word list	example sentence
1. _____	_____
2. _____	_____
3. _____	_____
4. _____	_____
5. _____	_____

Book 6: Prefix 'sub' – sentence matching

Go figure!

Can you figure out the meaning of these sentences? Cut out the boxes in the right column and match them to the boxes in the left column so that they make sense.

The fishing nets got tangled with	**subterranean** tunnel.
Hippos spend sixteen hours a day	of the continent of America.
The prisoners escaped through a	the **submarine**'s propeller.
The newsletter had many	**submerged** in rivers and lakes.
I **submitted** my application for	the angry protesters.
North America is a **subcontinent**	**submissive** posture.
The police managed to **subdue**	the money I owed my parents.
The dog lay on its back in a	a job at the museum.
When I got paid, I had to **subtract**	**subscribers**.

Book 6: Prefix 'sub' – word tree

Write the new words you have learned with the prefix 'sub' in the word tree.

sub = under, from below

Can you write a sentence for each of these words?

Book 6: Prefix 'super'

The prefix **'super'** comes from Latin and means 'over', 'above' or 'beyond'.

For example: **Super**man is a person with extraordinary powers, beyond those a normal human would have.

Draw a line from the words to the correct definitions.

superior — involving a speed greater than sound

superficial → higher in rank or quality

supersonic showing exceptional abilities or powers

supernatural occurring or existing on the surface

superhuman relating to something that can't be explained by the laws of nature (like a ghost)

Complete the diagram below.

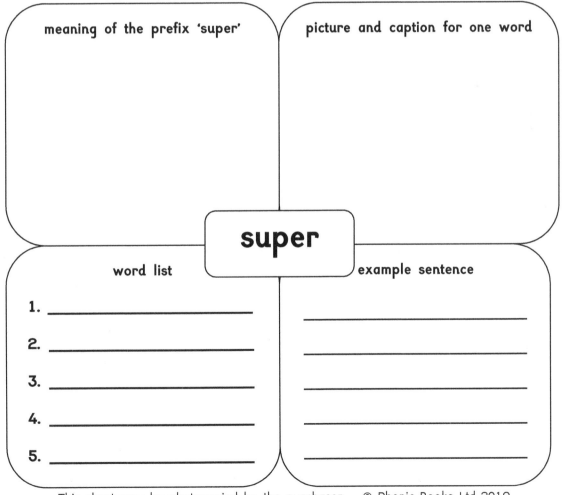

meaning of the prefix 'super'	picture and caption for one word

super

word list	example sentence
1. _____	_____
2. _____	_____
3. _____	_____
4. _____	_____
5. _____	_____

134

Book 6: Prefix 'super' – sentence matching

Go figure!

Can you figure out the meaning of these sentences? Cut out the boxes in the right column and match them to the boxes in the left column so that they make sense.

I grazed my knee, but the wound	comic published in America in 1938.
They needed **superhuman** effort	**supernatural** powers.
Superman is a **superhero** from a	workers in the factory.
My new bike is **superior** to my old	while they took their exam.
The teacher **supervised** the class	are **superstars**.
The **superintendent** oversees other	was not deep. It was **superficial**.
Many people believe in	bike because it has better gears.
In the US, basketball players	to swim to the distant shore.
Supersonic aircraft travel faster	than the speed of sound.

Book 6: Prefix 'super' – word tree

Write the new words you have learned with the prefix 'super' in the word tree.

super = over, above, beyond

Can you write a sentence for each of these words?

Book 6: Prefix 'trans'

The prefix **'trans'** comes from Latin and means 'across' or 'through'.

For example: to **trans**port something means to carry it from one place to another on a vehicle, ship or aircraft.

Draw a line from the words to the correct definitions.

transfer — the transfer of blood from one person to another

translate → to move from one place to another

transform you can see through it

transfusion to express words in another language

transparent to make a change in the nature, appearance or shape of something

Complete the diagram below.

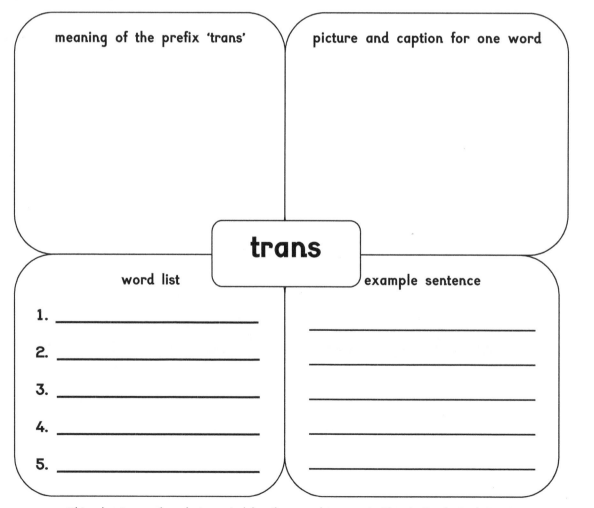

| meaning of the prefix 'trans' | picture and caption for one word |

trans

| word list | example sentence |

word list
1. _____
2. _____
3. _____
4. _____
5. _____

Book 6: Prefix 'trans' – sentence matching

Go figure!

Can you figure out the meaning of these sentences? Cut out the boxes in the right column and match them to the boxes in the left column so that they make sense.

The man lost so much blood he	light in as they are **translucent**.
To **transcribe** something is to	**translated** into many languages.
The first nonstop **transatlantic**	the beast **transforms** into a prince.
The windows must be **transparent**	to a better football club.
The Harry Potter books have been	use more public **transport**.
In the story 'Beauty and the Beast',	needed a **transfusion**.
Stained-glass windows let some	write something that is spoken.
The football player was **transferred**	so people can see through them.
To reduce pollution people must	flight took place in 1919.

Book 6: Prefix 'trans' – word tree

Write the new words you have learned with the prefix 'trans' in the word tree.

trans = across, through

Can you write a sentence for each of these words?

Book 6: Prefix 'inter'

The prefix **'inter'** comes from Latin and means 'between' or 'among'.

For example: **'inter**national' means 'occurring between nations'.

Draw a line from the words to the correct definitions.

interact — an electrical device that allows one-way or two-way communication

interrupt → to talk or do things with other people

intermission to stop a person speaking by saying something

interfere a short period between parts of a play or concert

intercom to involve yourself in a situation when your involvement is not wanted or helpful

Complete the diagram below.

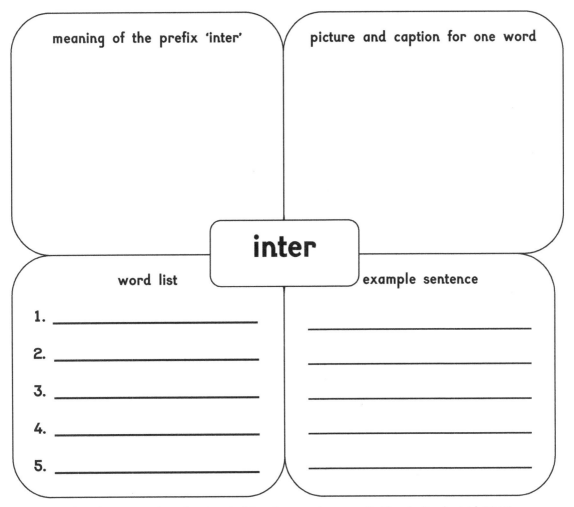

meaning of the prefix 'inter'

picture and caption for one word

inter

word list

1. _____

2. _____

3. _____

4. _____

5. _____

example sentence

_____

_____

_____

_____

_____

Book 6: Prefix 'inter' – sentence matching

Go figure!

Can you figure out the meaning of these sentences? Cut out the boxes in the right column and match them to the boxes in the left column so that they make sense.

The spy **intercepted** the message	all sign an **international** agreement.
The **internet** has changed the way	the **intercom**, we began to worry.
Interrupting is rude and people	hidden in the picture frame.
In the **intermission**, Mom bought	**intervened** to stop it.
It is best not to **interfere** in	engine began to turn.
When the old lady did not answer	should wait for their turn to speak.
The cogs **interlocked** and the	people communicate.
To save the environment, we must	matters that don't concern you.
There was a fight and the teacher	ice cream for everyone.

Book 6: Prefix 'inter' – word tree

Write the new words you have learned with the prefix 'inter' in the word tree.

inter = between, among

Can you write a sentence for each of these words?

Book 6: Prefix 'ex'

> The prefix **'ex'** comes from Latin and means 'out of'.
>
> For example: to **ex**clude someone is to keep them out.

Draw a line from the words to the correct definitions.

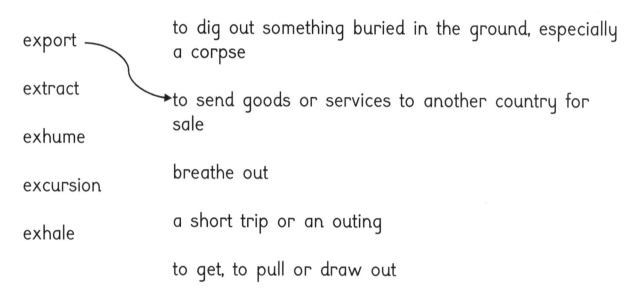

export   to dig out something buried in the ground, especially a corpse

extract   to send goods or services to another country for sale

exhume   breathe out

excursion   a short trip or an outing

exhale   to get, to pull or draw out

Complete the diagram below.

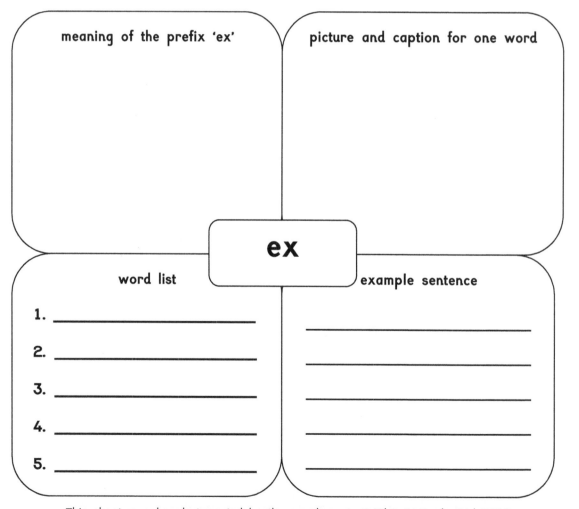

meaning of the prefix 'ex'

picture and caption for one word

ex

word list

1. _____
2. _____
3. _____
4. _____
5. _____

example sentence

_____
_____
_____
_____
_____

Book 6: Prefix 'ex' – sentence matching

Go figure!

Can you figure out the meaning of these sentences? Cut out the boxes in the right column and match them to the boxes in the left column so that they make sense.

The student was **expelled** from	Natural History Museum.
The dentist **extracted** the rotten	products than it **exports**.
The USA imports more	the school for bullying behavior.
The detective wanted the body	outgoing and socially confident.
We went on an **excursion** to the	tooth using a local anaesthetic.
Many people escaped from the	to **exhale** means to breathe out.
An **extrovert** is someone who is	a field, away from people.
Luckily, the bomb **exploded** in	cruel dictator and lived in **exile**.
To inhale means to breathe in and	**exhumed** from the grave.

144

Book 6: Prefix 'ex' – word tree

Write the new words you have learned with the prefix 'ex' in the word tree.

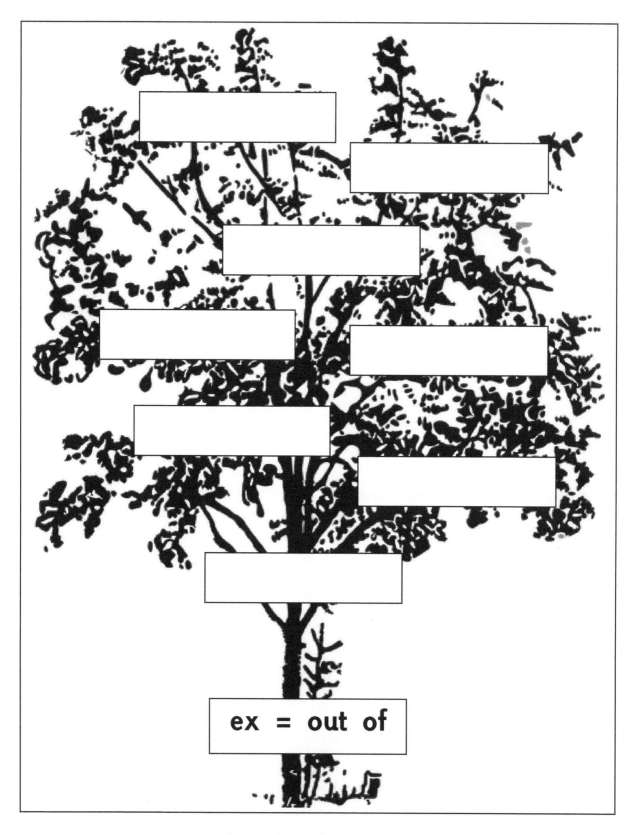

ex = out of

Can you write a sentence for each of these words?

Book 6: Prefixes 'sub', 'super', 'trans', 'inter', 'ex'

Insert these words into the text. Then reread the text to make sure it makes sense.

submerged interwoven extended exploring interrupted exposed transformed exotic transfixed transparent supernatural

The three friends spotted an (originating from a distant country) _______________ structure in the sea. It was partly (under water) _______________ in the sea. As the tide went out it emerged from the water. It was crumbling. It had been (uncovered, laid bare) _______________ to the elements for hundreds of years. As they were (investigating) _______________ it, there was a cracking sound. A huge crack opened. Izzy fell through a spiraling tunnel into an underground cavern below. When Kit and Finn joined her, they saw she was standing on a strange rocky island. This island had coils wrapped around it. They were covered in sticky, (see through) _______________ slime. This was no ordinary island. Their conversation was (broken up) _______________ by a mighty shudder. There was something (beyond natural) _______________ about it! The coils began to ripple. Izzy staggered. The orb tumbled from her pocket. It splashed into the waters below. Suddenly the rocks reared up and (changed form) _______________ into a living serpent! Kit and Izzy were (stood motionless) _______________ with horror.

Finn plunged into the water. He spotted the orb nestled in an (weaved together) _______________ net made of seaweed. Finn (held out) _______________ his hand and plucked it from the weeds.

Book 6: 4-in-a-row – 'sub', 'super', 'trans', 'inter', 'ex'

subtract	**super**star	**trans**late	**inter**rupt	**ex**hume
extrovert	**trans**mit	**inter**fere	**trans**fusion	**sub**marine
transparent	**ex**plode	**ex**tend	**super**vise	**sub**due
subjugate	**trans**fer	**trans**form	**ex**clude	**inter**act
intervene	**super**lative	**inter**cept	**ex**pel	**ex**ile
subscribe	**trans**lucent	**ex**port	**inter**face	**super**ior

Play with two sets of colored counters. Two players take turns to read the word and put a counter on the word. The winner is the first to get four of his/her counters in a row. The winner places a counter on the trophy cup above. The game is played four times until all the trophy cups are covered. Discuss new words with the student to help develop his/her vocabulary.

<u>Additional activities:</u> a) Ask the student to highlight the stress in the word so that he/she can learn to pronounce it correctly. b) Ask the student to split the words up into syllables.

Book 6: Revision 1: prefix – base/root word – suffix

Underline or highlight the base/root words. Then write the morphemes in the correct columns. For example: ex–port–ed.

ex port ed	expected	superhuman	interrupted
triangle	transformed	subscribe	previews
incredible	unicorn	transatlantic	submarine
predicted	expelled	interconnected	superstar

	prefix	base/root word	suffix
1	ex	port	ed
2			
3			
4			
5			
6			
7			
8			
9			
10			
11			
12			
13			
14			
15			
16			

Book 6: Revision 2: adding prefixes

Add the correct prefixes to the morphemes below.

Is it 'sub', 'super', 'trans', 'inter' or 'ex'?

	add prefix	base/root word	spelling		add prefix	base/root word	spelling
1	sub	marine	submarine	16		tract	
2		parent		17		plode	
3		rupt		18		lock	
4		net		19		press	
5		form		20		scribe	
6		ficial		21		fusion	
7		fer		22		marry	
8		national		23		pect	
9		clude		24		cept	
10		human		25		mit	
11		pel		26		ior	
12		merge		27		tract	
13		late		28		trovert	
14		port		29		hume	
15		fere		30		natural	

Correct your errors here:

_____

_____

Book 7: 'Facing Fears'

Contents

Book 7: Root words 'magna' and 'magni'

The root words **'magna'** and **'magni'** come from Latin and mean 'great'.

For example: **'magni**ficent' means 'made great'.

Draw a line from the words to the correct definitions.

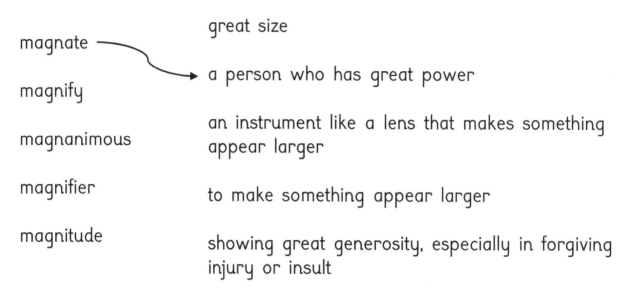

magnate   great size

                a person who has great power

magnify

                an instrument like a lens that makes something

magnanimous   appear larger

magnifier   to make something appear larger

magnitude   showing great generosity, especially in forgiving injury or insult

Complete the diagram below.

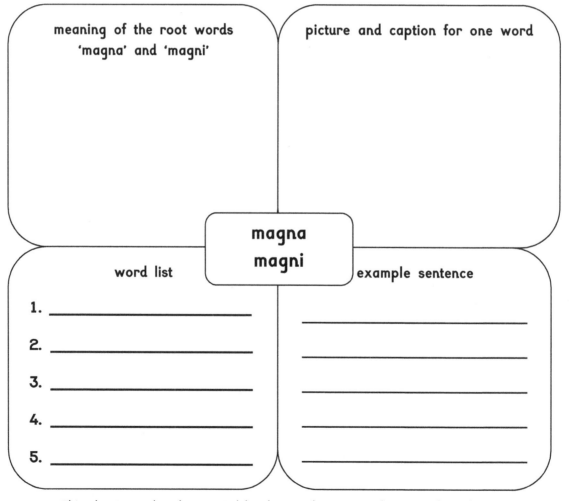

| meaning of the root words 'magna' and 'magni' | picture and caption for one word |

magna
magni

| word list | example sentence |

1. _____

2. _____

3. _____

4. _____

5. _____

Book 7: Root words 'magna' and 'magni' sentence matching

Go figure!

Can you figure out the meaning of these sentences? Cut out the boxes in the right column and match them to the boxes in the left column so that they make sense.

We used a **magnifying** glass	tower was **magnificent**.
The **magnate** donated millions	of the disaster.
People didn't realize the **magnitude**	to investigate the wing of an insect.
The view from the top of the	look many times larger.
To be **magnanimous** is to show	great generosity to others.
The **magnifier** made the seed	of dollars to charity.

Book 7: Root words 'magna' and 'magni' – word tree

Write the new words you have learned with the root words 'magna' and 'magni' in the word tree.

magna/magni = great

Can you write a sentence for each of these words?

Book 7: Prefix 'mega'

The prefix **'mega'** comes from Greek and means 'great' and 'large'.

For example: a **mega**star is someone who is very famous in the world of sport or entertainment.

Draw a line from the words to the correct definitions.

megalith

megabyte

megalomania

megaphone

megalosaurus

a large unit of computer memory

a large stone in a prehistoric structure (like Stonehenge)

a cone-shaped device that makes one's voice louder

a large carnivorous dinosaur from the mid-Jurassic period

an unnaturally strong wish for power and control

Complete the diagram below.

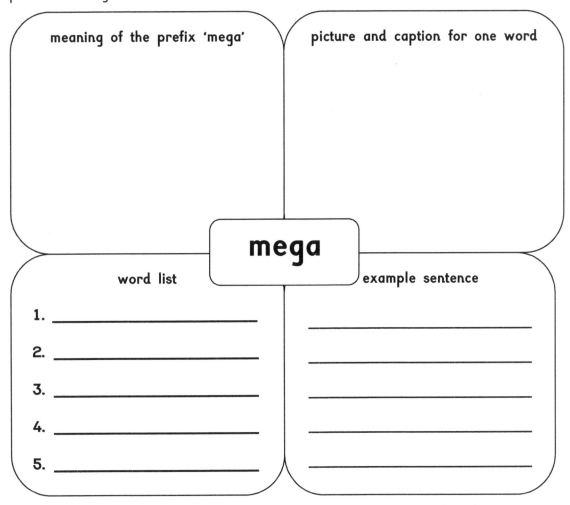

| meaning of the prefix 'mega' | picture and caption for one word |

mega

word list

1. _____

2. _____

3. _____

4. _____

5. _____

example sentence

_____

_____

_____

_____

_____

Book 7: Prefix 'mega' – sentence matching

Go figure!

Can you figure out the meaning of these sentences? Cut out the boxes in the right column and match them to the boxes in the left column so that they make sense.

The **megalosaurus** was a large	be heard above the noisy crowd.
This memory card holds 1	**megaliths** are placed in a circle.
The leader needed a **megaphone** to	band and now they are **megastars**.
Megalomania is an unnatural desire	a very large city.
No one knows exactly why these	carnivorous dinosaur.
'Megalopolis' is a Greek word for	to have power and control others.
Last year, no-one had heard of the	**megabyte** of memory.

Book 7: Prefix 'mega' – word tree

Write the new words you have learned with the prefix 'mega' in the word tree.

mega = great, large

Can you write a sentence for each of these words?

Book 7: Root word 'min' / Prefix 'mini'

The root word **'min'** and the prefix **'mini'** come from Latin and mean 'small' or 'less'. For example: **'mini**ature' means a very small version of something, such as a miniature painting.

Draw a line from the words to the correct definitions.

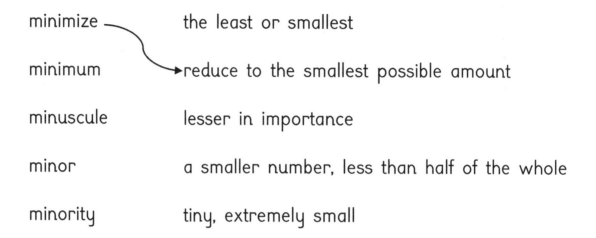

minimize — the least or smallest

minimum → reduce to the smallest possible amount

minuscule — lesser in importance

minor — a smaller number, less than half of the whole

minority — tiny, extremely small

Complete the diagram below.

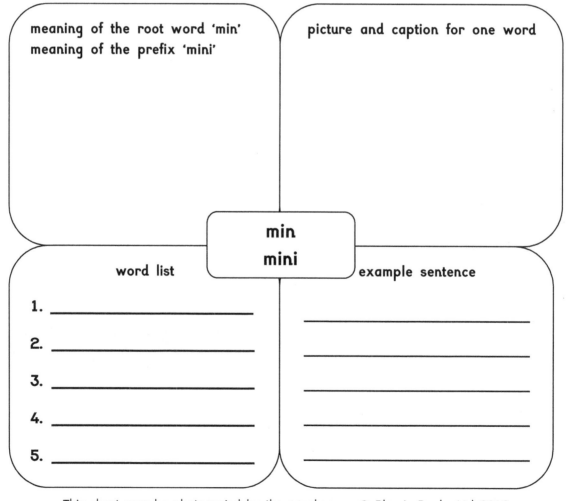

meaning of the root word 'min'
meaning of the prefix 'mini'

picture and caption for one word

min
mini

word list

1. _____
2. _____
3. _____
4. _____
5. _____

example sentence

_____
_____
_____
_____
_____

Book 7: Root word 'min' / Prefix 'mini' sentence matching

Go figure!

Can you figure out the meaning of these sentences? Cut out the boxes in the right column and match them to the boxes in the left column so that the sentences make sense.

As part of our **minibeasts** project,	furniture and **miniature** figures.
Minigolf is a fun game for	T.V. at home. A **minority** don't.
The doll's house has **miniature**	Luckily, no one got injured.
The **miniskirt** became fashionable	a **minimum** wage.
The majority of students have a	the whole family.
It was only a **minor** accident.	in the 1960's.
Everyone should be able to earn	we studied spiders and beetles.

Book 7: Root word 'min' / Prefix 'mini' – word tree

Write the new words you have learned with the root word 'min' and prefix 'mini' in the word tree.

min/mini = small, less

Can you write a sentence for each of these words?

Book 7: Prefix 'micro'

The prefix **'micro'** comes from Greek and means 'very small'.

For example: a **micro**scope is an instrument with lenses that magnify very small things and makes them look bigger.

Draw a line from the words to the correct definitions.

microchip   so small it can only be seen using a microscope

microwave   a small piece of silicon inside a computer

microscopic   a small community or place that reflects something bigger

microbe   a tiny organism, like bacteria

microcosm   an oven that uses waves of energy to cook or heat food quickly

Complete the diagram below.

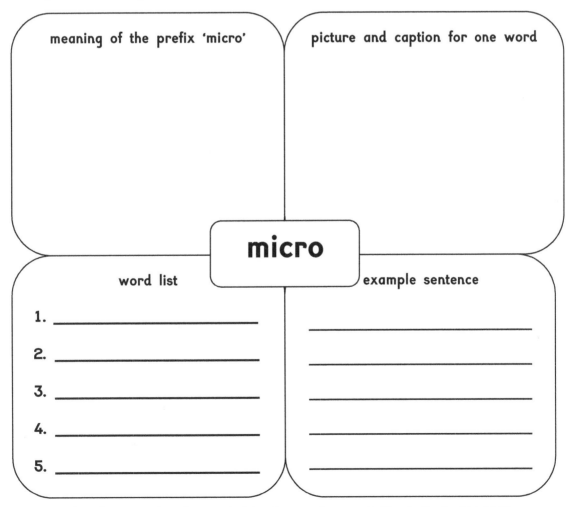

Book 7: Prefix 'micro' – sentence matching

Go figure!

Can you figure out the meaning of these sentences? Cut out the boxes in the right column and match them to the boxes in the left column so that the sentences make sense.

Mom said you mustn't put	can be found if he runs away.
A **microlight** is a very light, small	**microphone**.
My dog was **microchipped** so he	under the **microscope**.
The popstar sang into the	airplane for one or two people.
I plan to study **microbiology**	cause diseases.
The scientist studied the **microbes**	the metal dish in the **microwave**.
Germs are **microorganisms** that	at university.

Book 7: Prefix 'micro' – word tree

Write the new words you have learned with the prefix 'micro' in the word tree.

micro = small

Can you write a sentence for each of these words?

Book 7: 'magni', 'mega', 'min', 'mini', 'micro'

Insert these words into the text. Then reread the text to make sure it makes sense.

megastructure – a huge structure   **magnificent** – extremely impressive
minuscule – tiny   **diminish** – lessen
microscopic – very, very small   **minimal** – very small amount

As the Sea Dragon soared up into the sky, they looked down.
"That last monument looks tiny. It looks _____ from here!"
cried Kit. Izzy was anxious about Monk. He lay oddly quiet and still.
Finn was also worried. They were traveling through the clouds and the
Sea Dragon had ignored his question. Where were they?
Soon a startling vision appeared before them. They could see waterfalls
and a structure in the center. It was huge! It was a _____!
As they approached, they saw it was not a structure but a
_____ stone head. Now that it was clear where the next
monument was, Finn's worries began to _____.
The Sea Dragon circled in the air and landed skilfully on a rocky ledge
just above it. The three friends climbed carefully off. The Sea Dragon
did not speak. She gave them one last scornful look. With
_____ effort she leaped off the ledge and took to the skies.
"Where are we?" Izzy yelled after her. The Sea Dragon did not look
back. Soon she was just a tiny, _____ blue dot on the
horizon.

Book 7: 4-in-a-row – 'magna', 'magni', 'mega', 'min', 'mini', 'micro'

magnitude	**mega**star	**min**iature	**mini**bus	**micro**scope
microphone	**min**uscule	**mega**phone	**micro**chip	**mega**store
magnate	**mini**skirt	**magni**ficent	**min**or	**min**ority
megabyte	**mini**bus	**micro**light	**mega**lith	**mega**dose
minibike	di**min**ish	**magn**ify	**min**imize	**min**imum
megastar	**micro**wave	**min**ute	**min**imal	**mini**golf

Play with two sets of colored counters. Two players take turns to read the word and put a counter on the word. The winner is the first to get four of his/her counters in a row. The winner places a counter on the trophy cup above. The game is played four times until all the trophy cups are covered. Discuss new words with the student to help develop his/her vocabulary.

<u>Additional activities</u>: a) Ask the student to highlight the stress in the word so that he/she can learn to pronounce it correctly. b) Ask the student to split the words up into syllables.

Book 7: Revision 1: prefix – base/root word – suffix

Underline or highlight the base/root words. Then write the morphemes in the correct columns. For example: re-mind-ed.

	re mind ed	microphone	retreated	megastore
	extended	magnify	minimum	interact
	impossible	minibus	disappeared	megalith
	explained	microwave	interfere	microorganism

	prefix	base/root word	suffix
1	re	mind	ed
2			
3			
4			
5			
6			
7			
8			
9			
10			
11			
12			
13			
14			
15			
16			

Book 7: Revision 2: adding prefixes / root words

Add the correct prefixes or root words to the morphemes below.

Is it 'magna', 'magni', 'mega', 'min', 'mini' or 'micro'?

	add prefix/ root word		spelling		add prefix/ root word		spelling
1	mega	hit	megahit	16		te	
2		fy		17		nimous	
3		bus		18		uscule	
4		golf		19		ature	
5		wave		20		mize	
6		byte		21		fier	
7		chip		22		dose	
8		scope		23		computer	
9		biology		24		losaurus	
10		phone		25		lith	
11		bike		26		cab	
12		ficent		27		light	
13		chip		28		tude	
14		star		29		cosm	
15		lomania		30		mal	

Correct your errors here:

_____

_____

This sheet may be photocopied by the purchaser. © Phonic Books Ltd 2019

Book 8: 'Bounty in the Lagoon'

Contents

Book 8: Root words 'cap' and 'capit'

The root words **'cap'** and **'capit'** come from Latin and mean 'head'.

For example: A **capit**al city is the place where the government sits.   It is the 'head city' of a country or state.

Draw a line from the words to the correct definitions.

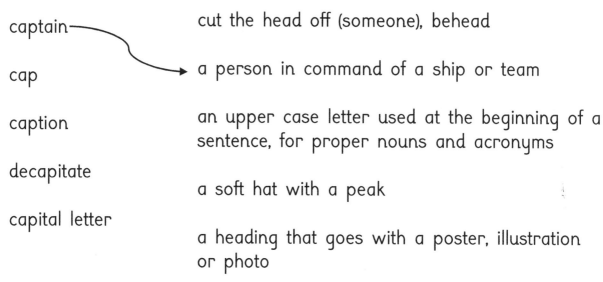

captain   cut the head off (someone), behead

cap   a person in command of a ship or team

caption   an upper case letter used at the beginning of a sentence, for proper nouns and acronyms

decapitate   a soft hat with a peak

capital letter   a heading that goes with a poster, illustration or photo

Complete the diagram below.

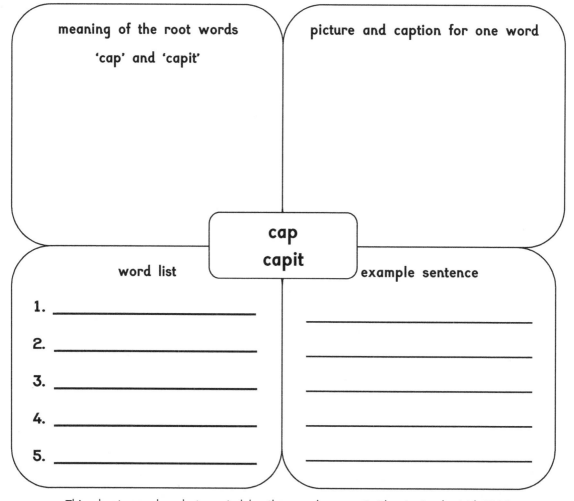

meaning of the root words 'cap' and 'capit'

picture and caption for one word

cap
capit

word list

1. _____

2. _____

3. _____

4. _____

5. _____

example sentence

_____

_____

_____

_____

_____

Book 8: Root word 'man'

The root word **'man'** comes from Latin and means 'hand'.

For example: **Man**ual labor is physical work done by men or women (not done by machines or animals). It is work that is done with the hands, such as brick–laying.

Draw a line from the words to the correct definitions.

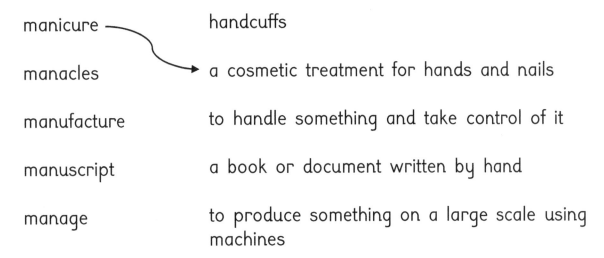

manicure   handcuffs

manacles   a cosmetic treatment for hands and nails

manufacture   to handle something and take control of it

manuscript   a book or document written by hand

manage   to produce something on a large scale using machines

Complete the diagram below.

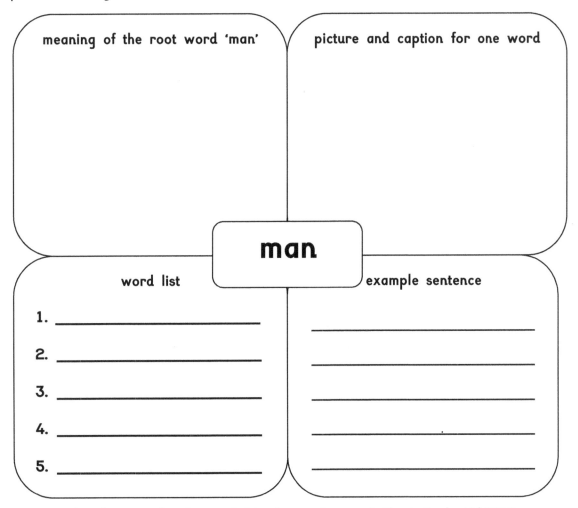

meaning of the root word 'man'

picture and caption for one word

man

word list

1. _____

2. _____

3. _____

4. _____

5. _____

example sentence

_____

_____

_____

_____

_____

Book 8: Root word 'spect'

The root word **'spect'** comes from Latin and means 'see'.

For example: **Spect**acles are glasses that help us to see.

Draw a line from the words to the correct definitions.

inspect   a person who watches a show, game or event

respect   to look at something closely and critically

suspect   a point of view

spectator   to believe someone is guilty of a crime

perspective   to admire someone

Complete the diagram below.

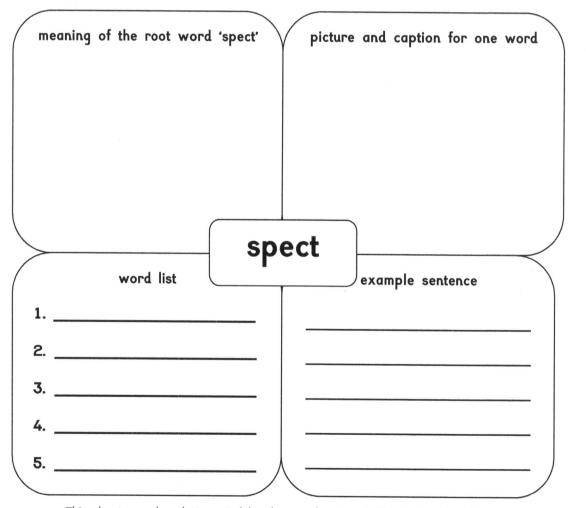

Book 8: Root word 'ped'

The root word **'ped'** comes from Latin and means 'foot'.

For example: **Ped**als are levers that you push with your feet when you ride a bicycle.

Draw a line from the words to the correct definitions.

pedestrian — an animal that walks on two feet

biped → a person who travels on foot

centipede — an instrument that records the number of steps taken

expedition — an arthropod that has many segments, each with a pair of legs

pedometer — a journey or voyage to discover new places or things

Complete the diagram below.

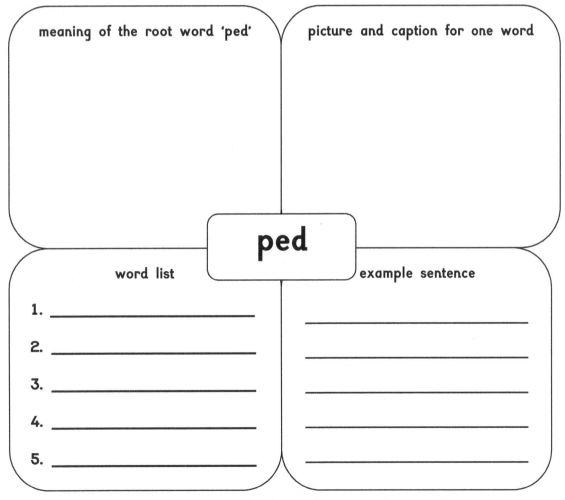

meaning of the root word 'ped'

picture and caption for one word

ped

word list

1. _____
2. _____
3. _____
4. _____
5. _____

example sentence

_____
_____
_____
_____
_____

172

Book 8: Root words 'cap', 'capit', 'man', 'spect' and 'ped'

cap, capit = head

cap

capital

caption

decapitate

capital letter

spect = see

spectacles

inspect

inspector

respect

suspect

spectator

man = hand

ma<u>ni</u>cure

manage

manual

manufacture

manacles

ped = foot

pedals

biped

quadruped

pedestrian

centipede

expedition

Underline the root words in the lists. Discuss the words and their meaning. Can you guess how they are connected to the root within them? Use these words to complete the cloze activity on the next page.

This sheet may be photocopied by the purchaser. © Phonic Books Ltd 2019

Book 8: Root words: 'cap', 'capit', 'man', 'spect' and 'ped'

Use the words from the previous page to complete these sentences.

---

capit = head (from Latin)

1. A city where the government of the country sits is the _____ city.
2. A soft flat hat is called a _____.
3. An upper case letter is also called a _____.
4. To _____ means to cut the head off.

---

man = hand (from Latin)

1. A cosmetic treatment for nails is called a _____.
2. Handcuffs are also called _____.
3. To _____ something is to handle it and take control of it.
4. To work with your hands is called _____ work.

---

spect = see, look at (from Latin)

1. To think that someone is guilty of something is to _____ him or her.
2. _____ is another word for glasses.
3. To admire someone is to _____ him or her.
4. Someone who watches a football match is a _____.

---

ped = foot (from Latin)

1. A _____ is an animal that walks on two feet.
2. When you ride a bicycle, you push the _____ with your feet.
3. A person who travels on foot is a _____.
4. A journey to discover new places is called an _____.

174

Book 8: Root words 'cap', 'capit', 'man', 'spect' and 'ped'

cap, capit = head

spect = see

man = hand

ped = foot

Write the words you have learned with the roots: 'cap', 'capit', 'man', 'spect' and 'ped' in the correct boxes. Now choose two words from each box and write a sentence for each word.

Book 8: 4-in-a-row – 'cap', 'capit', 'man', 'spect', 'ped'

captain	**man**acles	**spect**acle	**ped**al	re**spect**
manicure	**spect**acular	**man**ual	**ped**estrian	**cap**
bi**ped**	**spect**acles	ex**ped**ition	**man**age	**cap**tion
quadru**ped**	**man**ufacture	de**capit**ate	**capit**al	in**spect**
su**spect**	in**spect**ion	**man**ager	**spect**ator	centi**ped**e
pedometer	per**spect**ive	**capit**alism	in**spect**or	**man**uscript

Play with two sets of colored counters. Two players take turns to read the word and put a counter on the word. The winner is the first to get four of his/her counters in a row. The winner places a counter on the trophy cup above. The game is played four times until all the trophy cups are covered. Discuss new words with the student to help develop his/her vocabulary.

Additional activities: a) Ask the student to highlight the stress in the word so that he/she can learn to pronounce it correctly. b) Ask the student to split the words up into syllables.

Book 8: Root word 'bio'

> The root word **'bio'** comes from Greek and means 'life'.
>
> For example: **Bio**logy is the study of living things such as plants and animals.

Draw a line from the words to the correct definitions.

biography   something that can be broken down slowly by natural processes

biodegradable   a story of someone's life written by someone else

biodiversity   an animal such as a frog that can live on land and in water

autobiography

amphibian   the variety of life

                    a story of someone's life written by that person

Complete the diagram below.

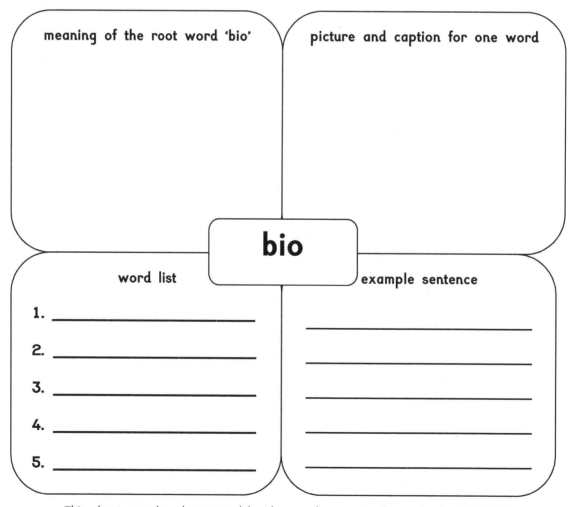

- meaning of the root word 'bio'
- picture and caption for one word
- **bio**
- word list
  1. _____
  2. _____
  3. _____
  4. _____
  5. _____
- example sentence

Book 8: Root words 'viv' and 'vit'

The root words **viv** and **vit** come from Latin and mean 'life'.

For example: To re**vive** someone means to bring him/her back to life.

Draw a line from the words to the correct definitions.

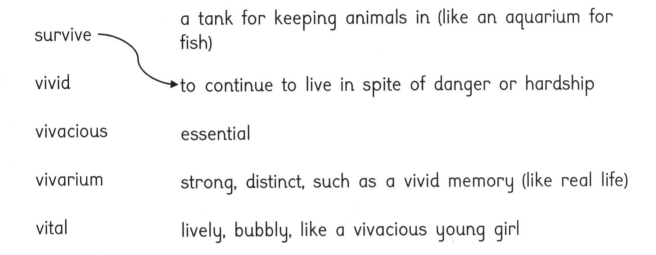

survive   a tank for keeping animals in (like an aquarium for fish)

vivid   to continue to live in spite of danger or hardship

vivacious   essential

vivarium   strong, distinct, such as a vivid memory (like real life)

vital   lively, bubbly, like a vivacious young girl

Complete the diagram below.

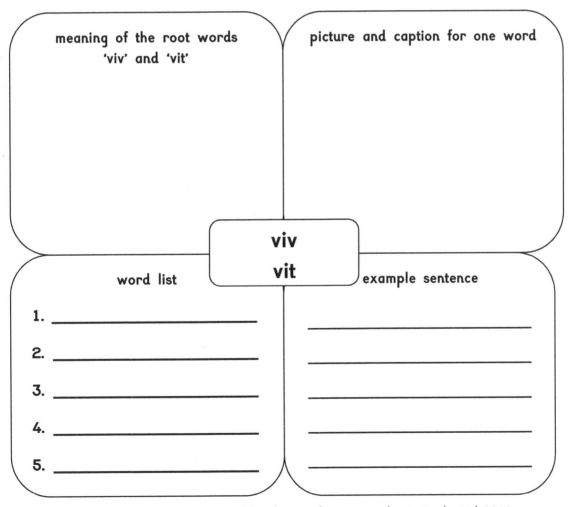

meaning of the root words 'viv' and 'vit'

picture and caption for one word

viv

vit

word list

1. _____

2. _____

3. _____

4. _____

5. _____

example sentence

_____

_____

_____

_____

_____

Book 8: Root word 'mort'

The root word **'mort'** comes from Latin and means 'death'.

For example: To be **mort**al is to be human and to die at the end of one's life.

Draw a line from the words to the correct definitions.

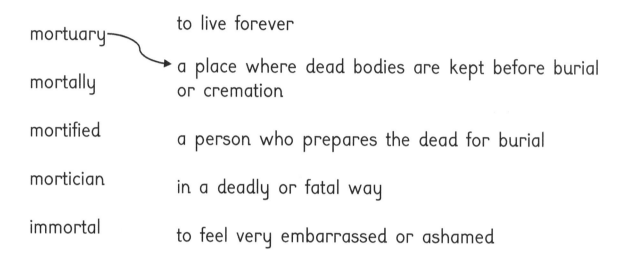

mortuary — to live forever

a place where dead bodies are kept before burial or cremation

mortally

mortified — a person who prepares the dead for burial

mortician — in a deadly or fatal way

immortal — to feel very embarrassed or ashamed

Complete the diagram below.

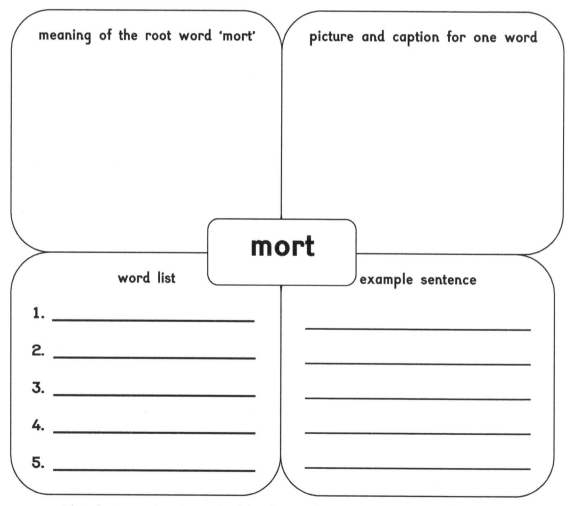

meaning of the root word 'mort'

picture and caption for one word

mort

word list

1. _____

2. _____

3. _____

4. _____

5. _____

example sentence

_____

_____

_____

_____

_____

Book 8: Root words 'bio', 'viv', 'vit', 'mort' – revision

WANTED DEAD OR ALIVE!

bio = life
(from Greek)

biology
biography
autobiography
biodiversity
biodegradable
amphibian

viv, vit = life
(from Latin)

revive
survive
vital
vivid
vivarium
vivacious

mort = dead
(from Latin)

mortal
immortal
mortician
postmortem
mortified
mortuary

Use these words to complete the missing words in the cloze activity on the next page. © Phonic Books Ltd 2019

This sheet may be photocopied by the purchaser.

Book 8: Root words: 'bio', 'viv', 'vit', 'mort'

Use the words from the previous page to complete these sentences.

---

bio = life (from Greek)

1. Plastic is not a _____ material.

2. A _____ is a written account of someone's life.

3. An _____ can live both on land and in water.

4. _____ means a variety of plant and animal life in a certain habitat.

5. _____ is the study of living things.

6. When I grow old, I will write an _____ of my life.

---

viv/vit = life (from Latin)

1. A _____ is an enclosure where animals are kept.

2. To be _____ is to behave in a lively way.

3. It is _____ to take water when walking in the desert.

4. Many people _____ed the earthquake.

5. The old man had _____ memories of his childhood.

6. The patient was _____ed in casualty.

---

mort = death (from Latin)

1. A _____ examination showed that the man died of a heart attack.

2. I was _____ when I slipped on the dance floor in front of everyone.

3. The body of the dead man lay in the _____.

4. The _____ prepared the body for burial.

5. The Greek gods were _____.

6. Humans don't live forever because they are _____.

Book 8: Root words 'bio', 'viv', 'vit', 'mort' – revision

WANTED DEAD OR ALIVE!

bio = life
(from Greek)

viv, vit = life
(from Latin)

mort = dead
(from Latin)

Write words with the roots: 'bio', 'viv', 'vit' and 'mort' in the correct columns. Choose two words from each column and write a sentence for each word.

Book 8: 'capit', 'man', 'spect', 'bio', 'viv', 'mort'

Insert these words into the text. Then reread the text to make sure it makes sense.

perspective – point of view

capital – head city

managed – was able to

survived – continued to live

mortally – could have died

decapitated – head cut off

biodiversity – variety of life in a habitat

vivid – strong

amphibian – animal that lives both on land and in water

Racing down to earth on the back of a giant _____ – an Aquareon – was both exciting and terrifying. Soon they spotted a vast city! From above, they had an amazing _____ of the city. It looked like a _____ city, but as they approached, they saw it was deserted.

"Look at that!" yelled Kit. "There, by the harbor! It's a giant warrior." The Aquareon flew right through its massive legs. Izzy closed her eyes in terror. She thought they were going to be _____. She just about _____ to stay on the back of the Aquareon. The Aquareon soared onwards. Soon they were flying over a lush tropical forest. Izzy saw the _____ colors of green and blue. Beneath them was a maze of rivers. What a wonderful _____ of nature! Plants overhung the fast-flowing waterways. The Aquareon dived down, aiming straight at the water.

"Jump!" yelled Kit. The three friends leaped off the Guardian's back just as it crashed into the water. They resurfaced, gasping for air. They could have died from the crash or they could have been _____ wounded! Luckily, the three friends _____.

Book 8: 4-in-a-row – 'bio', 'viv', 'vit', 'mort'

biology	**vit**al	**mort**al	**mort**ality	amphi**bi**an
sur**viv**e	**bio**graphy	**mort**ician	**viv**id	post**mort**em
vivacious	**mort**ally	**mort**ify	sur**viv**al	**mort**uary
morgue	**viv**arium	im**mort**al	**bio**psy	im**mort**ality
biodiversity	re**viv**ed	**mort**gage	auto-**bio**graphy	**bio**-degradable
vitality	sur**viv**or	sur**viv**al	**mor**ibund	re**vit**alize

Play with two sets of colored counters. Two players take turns to read the word and put a counter on the word. The winner is the first to get four of his/her counters in a row. The winner places a counter on the trophy cup above. The game is played four times until all the trophy cups are covered. Discuss new words with the student to help develop his/her vocabulary.

<u>Additional activities</u>: a) Ask the student to highlight the stress in the word so that he/she can learn to pronounce it correctly. b) Ask the student to split the words up into syllables.

Book 8: Revision: prefix – root word – suffix

Underline or highlight the root words. Then write the morphemes in the correct columns. For example: re–spect–ed.

	re spect ed	biology	revive	survivor
	manacles	capital	immortal	centipede
	pedals	biped	perspective	spectacles
	manage	inspection	pedlar	decapitate

	prefix	root word	suffix
1	re	spect	ed
2			
3			
4			
5			
6			
7			
8			
9			
10			
11			
12			
13			
14			
15			
16			

Book 9: 'Sounds of the Sirens'

Contents

Book 9: Root word 'dict'

> The root word **'dict'** comes from Latin and it means 'say'.
>
> For example: The word **'dict**ate' can mean 'to give an order' or 'to say words that are written down'.

Draw a line from the words to the correct definitions.

predict   a book that lists words and their meanings

dictator   to say what will happen in the future

dictionary   the act of speaking words that are written down by someone else

contradict   a ruler with total power over a country

dictation   to say the opposite

Complete the diagram below.

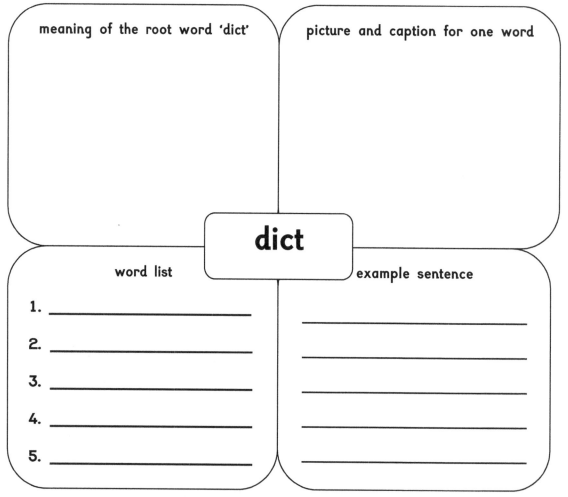

meaning of the root word 'dict'	picture and caption for one word

dict

word list	example sentence
1. _____	_____
2. _____	_____
3. _____	_____
4. _____	_____
5. _____	_____

Book 9: Root word 'dict' – sentence matching

Go figure!

Can you figure out the meaning of these sentences? Cut out the boxes in the right column and match them to the boxes in the left column so that the sentences make sense.

A **dictator** is a ruler who has total	say the opposite of what they said.
The teacher gives the class a	or command made by a king.
The actor didn't speak clearly,	control and power of a country.
To **contradict** someone is to	an online **dictionary**.
'Bene' means 'good', so the word	spelling **dictation** every Friday.
Nowadays, students prefer to use	**'benediction'** means 'a blessing'.
An **edict** is an announcement	rain on the weekend.
The weather man **predicted**	so she had to improve her **diction**.

Book 9: Root word 'dict' – word tree

Write the new words you have learned with the root word 'dict' in the word tree.

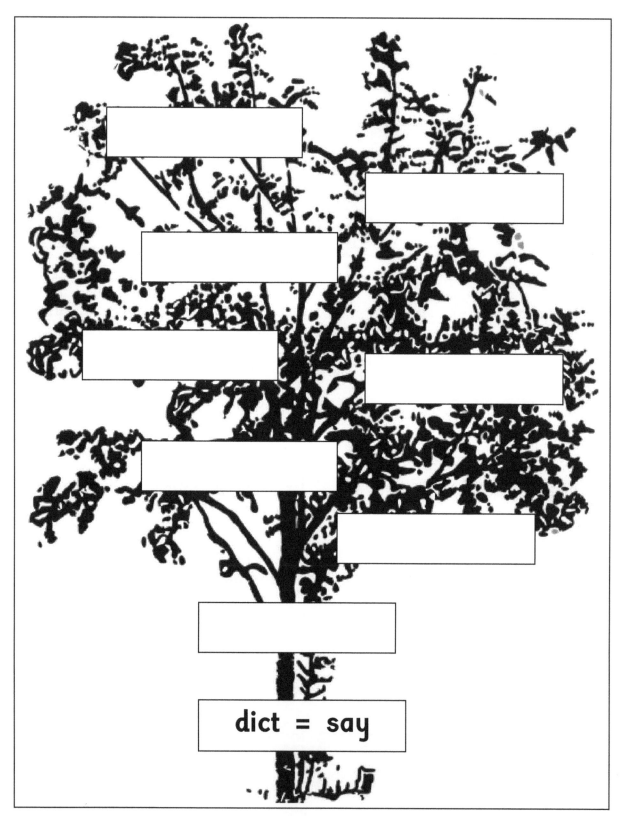

dict = say

Can you write a sentence for each of these words?

Book 9: Root word 'graph'

> The root word 'graph' comes from Greek and it means 'to write'.
>
> For example: The word bio**graph**y means the written story of someone's life.

Draw a line from the words to the correct definitions.

autograph   a picture made using a camera

paragraph   → a signature, especially one written by a celebrity for a fan

photograph   a chart or diagram

graph   a list of books that are mentioned in a book

bibliography   a unit of writing, usually a few sentences about one central idea

Complete the diagram below.

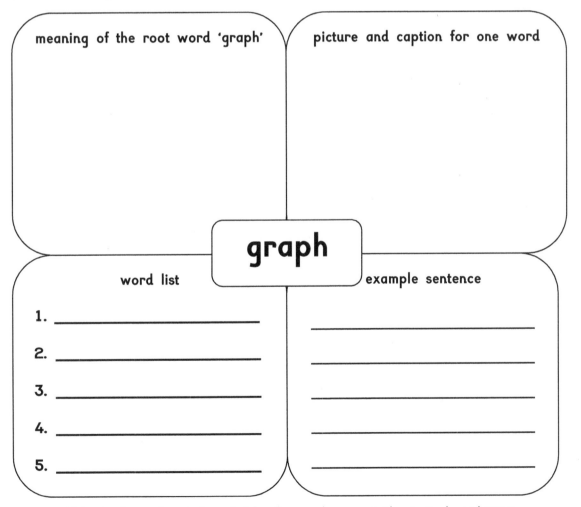

meaning of the root word 'graph'	picture and caption for one word

graph

word list	example sentence
1. _____	_____
2. _____	_____
3. _____	_____
4. _____	_____
5. _____	_____

190

Book 9: Root word 'graph' – sentence matching

Go figure!

Can you figure out the meaning of these sentences? Cut out the boxes in the right column and match them to the boxes in the left column so that the sentences make sense.

Geography is the study of the	written by someone famous.
Cartography is the study of the	of a person's life.
A **paragraph** is a unit of text	Earth's surface, climate and peoples.
A **graph** is a diagram that shows	drawing of maps.
An **autograph** is a signature usually	Minister wrote an **autobiography**.
A **biography** is a written account	by a camera.
A **photograph** is a picture made	centered on one idea.
After she retired, the Prime	information is a visual way.

Book 9: Root word 'graph' – word tree

Write the new words you have learned with the root word 'graph' in the word tree.

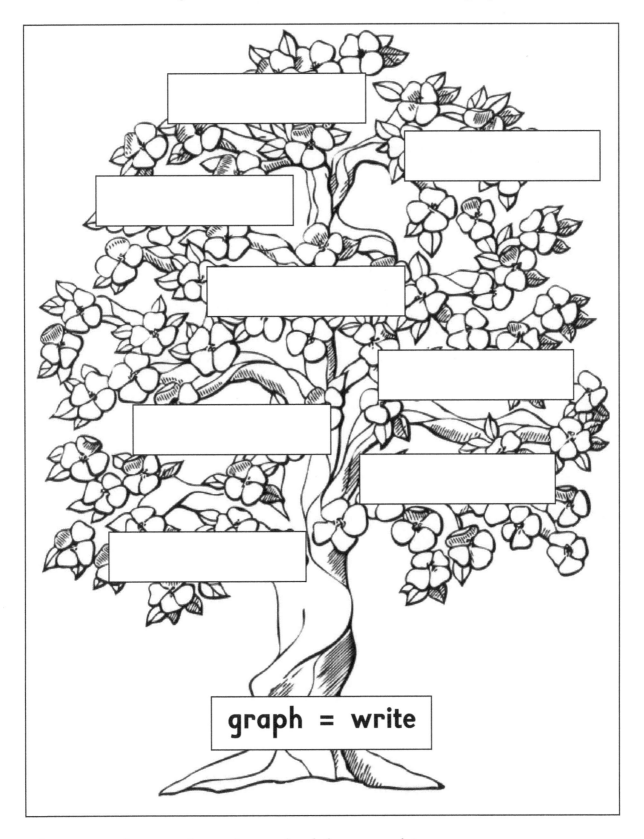

graph = write

Can you write a sentence for each of these words?

 © Phonic Books Ltd 2019

Book 9: Root words 'scrib' and 'script'

The root words **'scrib'** and **'script'** come from Latin and mean 'write'.

For example: The word 'de**scribe**' means 'write down'.

Draw a line from the words to the correct definitions.

scribble

subscribe

prescription

manuscript

postscript

a book or document of music written by hand

to write something in a careless or hurried way

P.S. – an additional remark added to the end of a letter

an instruction written by a doctor ordering treatment for the patient

to sign up for something and receive it on a regular basis

Complete the diagram below.

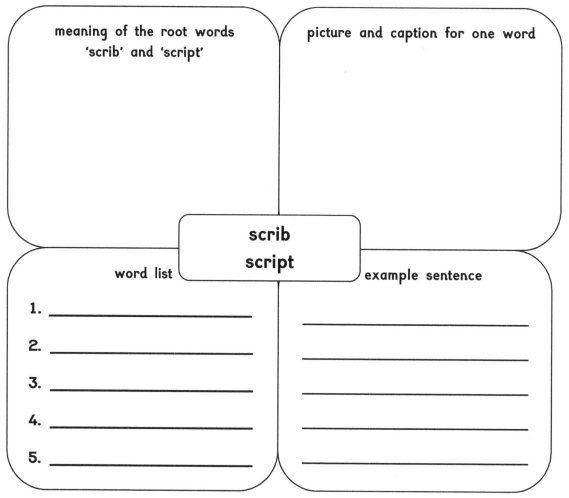

meaning of the root words 'scrib' and 'script'

picture and caption for one word

scrib

script

word list

example sentence

1. _____

2. _____

3. _____

4. _____

5. _____

_____

_____

_____

_____

_____

Book 9: Root words 'scrib' and 'script' – word tree

Write the words you have learned with the root words 'scrib' and 'script' in the word tree.

scrib, script = write

Can you write a sentence for each of these words?

Book 9: Root word 'mem'

The root word **'mem'** comes from Latin and it means 'bring to mind'.

For example: The word **'mem**orable' means 'an experience that is easily remembered'.

Draw a line from the words to the correct definitions.

remember   a monument built to remind people of a person or an event

memo   to bring to one's mind, recall, recollect

memoir   objects that are collected to remind one of people or events

memorial   a biography or historical account written from personal knowledge

memorabilia

a short written message from one part of an organization to another

Complete the diagram below.

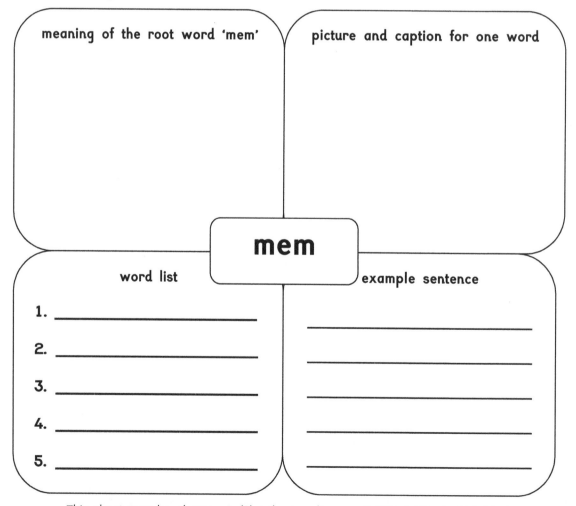

Book 9: Root word 'mem' – sentence matching

Go figure!

Can you figure out the meaning of these sentences? Cut out the boxes in the right column and match them to the boxes in the left column so that the sentences make sense.

The boss sent out a **memo** to let	two, when I was stung by a bee.
My first **memory** goes back to age	everyone know about the meeting.
Every year we **commemorate**	there from time **immemorial**.
When the Prime Minister retires,	she will write her **memoirs**.
My father collects **memorabilia** of	a war **memorial** for World War I.
My class traveled to France to visit	the soldiers who died in the wars.
Stonehenge has been standing	his favorite football team.

Book 9: Root word 'mem' – word tree

Write the new words you have learned with the root word 'mem' in the word tree.

mem = bring to mind

Can you write a sentence for each of these words?

Book 9: 'dict', 'graph', 'scrib', 'script', 'mem'

Insert these words into the text. Then reread the text to make sure it makes sense.

described – gave a detailed account of   **remembered** – recalled

contradict – say the opposite   **predicted** – foretold

memories – things recalled from the past

topography – physical features of the local area

"The next Guardian will be in that huge monument, in the town we flew past!" Finn _____.

"That's the Port of Yaneth. You'll have to go by sea if you want to get there," Pablo said. Pablo drew a quick sketch of a map in the sand. He _____ to the others the _____ of the area. "The quickest way is by boat," he explained. "Let me help you make a coracle."

Pablo showed them how to weave bamboo into a watertight coracle. By midday, the boat was ready to take them back upriver to the Port of Yaneth.

"Where's Monk?" asked Finn as they prepared to set sail.

"I think Monk may be needed here, Finn," said Izzy softly.

Finn's heart sank. He wanted to _____ her, but he knew that Monk had decided to stay. He _____ all the amazing adventures they had experienced together. He would cherish those _____ for the rest of his life. Monk gave Finn a quick hug and turned to hold Shumi's hand. As they paddled away, Finn looked on sadly as Shumi and Monk turned and walked away.

Book 9: 4-in-a-row – 'dict', 'graph', 'scrib', 'script', 'mem'

dictation	**graph**	de**scrib**e	tran**scrib**e	**mem**oir
in**scrib**e	**bio**graphy	**dict**ator	**graph**ic	geo**graph**y
pre**dict**	manu**script**	**script**ure	pre**script**ion	pre**dict**ion
scribble	auto**graph**	de**script**ion	bio**graph**y	**dict**ionary
post**script**	**mem**o	contra**dict**	auto-bio**graph**y	im**mem**orial
bene**dict**ion	e**dict**	**scrib**e	sub**scrib**e	re**mem**ber

Play with two sets of colored counters. Two players take turns to read the word and put a counter on the word. The winner is the first to get four of his/her counters in a row. The winner places a counter on the trophy cup above. The game is played four times until all the trophy cups are covered. Discuss new words with the student to help develop his/her vocabulary.

Additional activities: a) Ask the student to highlight the stress in the word so that he/she can learn to pronounce it correctly. b) Ask the student to split the words up into syllables.

Book 9: Revision: prefix – root word – suffix

Underline or highlight the root words. Then write the morphemes in the correct columns. For example: pre-<u>dict</u>-ed.

pre <u>dict</u> ed	contradicted	geography	autograph
manuscript	prescription	dictate	remember
memoir	biography	scripture	subscribe
edict	inscribe	paragraph	describing

	prefix	root word	suffix
1	pre	dict	ed
2			
3			
4			
5			
6			
7			
8			
9			
10			
11			
12			
13			
14			
15			
16			

Book 10: 'Guardians Unite'

Contents

Book 10: Root word 'ject'

The root word '**ject**' comes from Latin and means 'throw'.

For example: to re**ject** something means, literally, 'to throw it back'.

Draw a line from the words to the correct definitions.

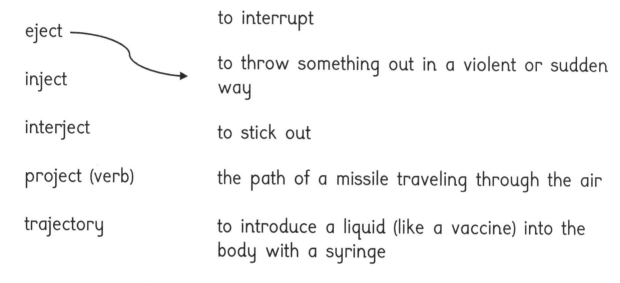

eject

inject

interject

project (verb)

trajectory

to interrupt

to throw something out in a violent or sudden way

to stick out

the path of a missile traveling through the air

to introduce a liquid (like a vaccine) into the body with a syringe

Complete the diagram below.

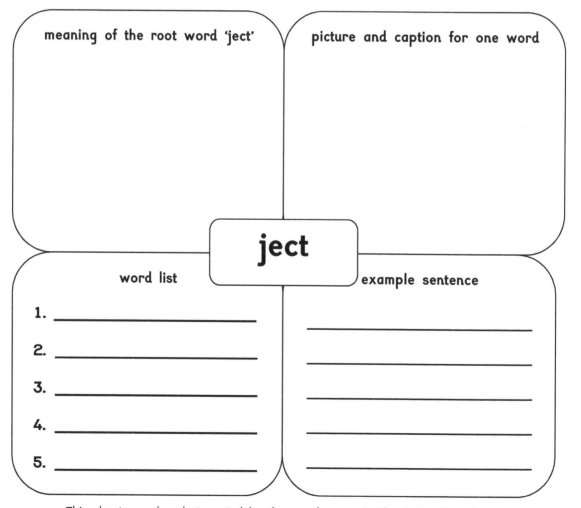

meaning of the root word 'ject'

picture and caption for one word

ject

word list

1. _____

2. _____

3. _____

4. _____

5. _____

example sentence

_____

_____

_____

_____

_____

Book 10: Root word 'tract'

The root word **'tract'** comes from Latin and means 'pull' or 'drag'.

For example: to ex**tract** a tooth means 'to pull a tooth out'.

Draw a line from the words to the correct definitions.

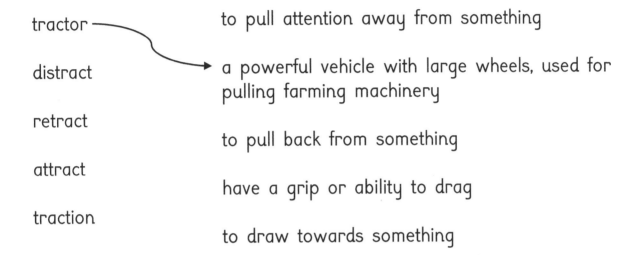

tractor   to pull attention away from something

distract   a powerful vehicle with large wheels, used for
                            pulling farming machinery

retract   to pull back from something

attract   have a grip or ability to drag

traction   to draw towards something

Complete the diagram below.

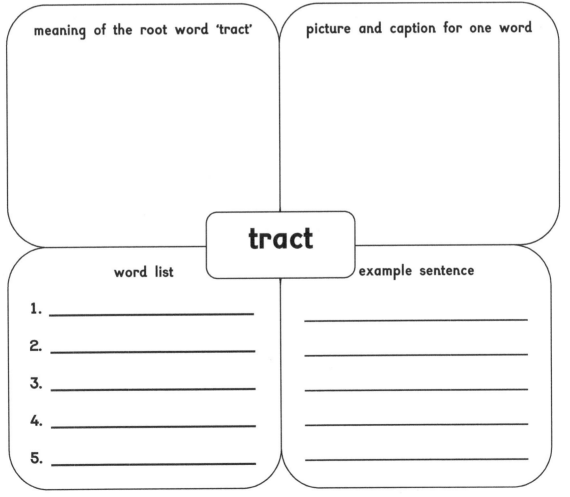

meaning of the root word 'tract'	picture and caption for one word

tract

word list	example sentence
1. _____	_____
2. _____	_____
3. _____	_____
4. _____	_____
5. _____	_____

Book 10: Root word 'port'

The root word **'port'** comes from Latin and means 'carry'.

For example: a **port**able chair is a chair that you can carry.

Draw a line from the words to the correct definitions.

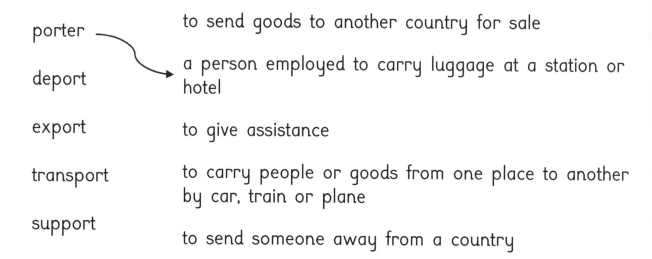

porter — to send goods to another country for sale

deport → a person employed to carry luggage at a station or hotel

export — to give assistance

transport — to carry people or goods from one place to another by car, train or plane

support — to send someone away from a country

Complete the diagram below.

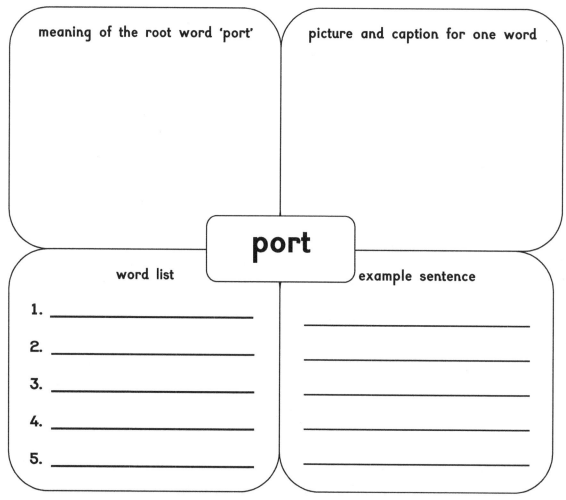

meaning of the root word 'port'

picture and caption for one word

port

word list

1. _____
2. _____
3. _____
4. _____
5. _____

example sentence

Book 10: Root word 'struct'

The root word **'struct'** comes from Latin and means 'pile up' or 'build'.

For example: the word 'con**struct**' means 'build or heap together'.

Draw a line from the words to the correct definitions.

structure   to tell someone to do something or to teach a subject or skill

restructure   something built, like a building, bridge or dam

construction   to organize differently

destruction   the action of building

instruct   the act of destroying

Complete the diagram below.

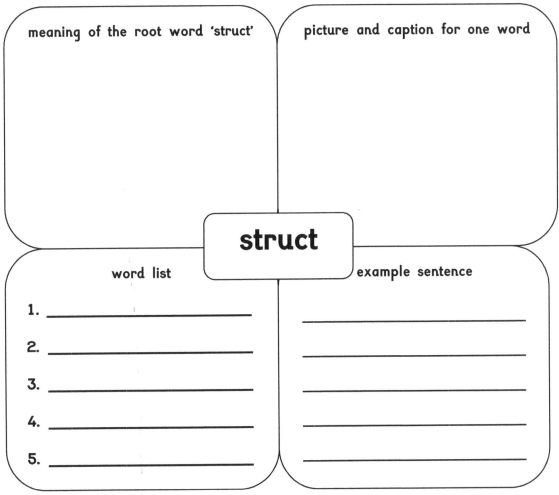

meaning of the root word 'struct'

picture and caption for one word

struct

word list

1. _____

2. _____

3. _____

4. _____

5. _____

example sentence

_____

_____

_____

_____

_____

Book 10: Root words 'ject', 'tract', 'port', 'struct'

GET ACTIVE IN LATIN!

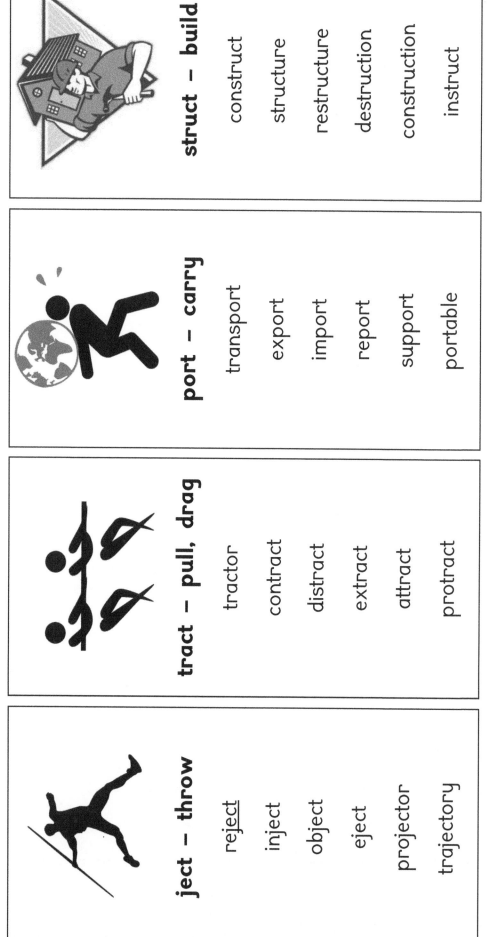

ject – throw

reject

inject

object

eject

projector

trajectory

tract – pull, drag

tractor

contract

distract

extract

attract

protract

port – carry

transport

export

import

report

support

portable

struct – build

construct

structure

restructure

destruction

construction

instruct

Underline the root words in the lists above. Discuss the words and their meaning. Can you guess how they are connected to the root within them? Use these words to complete the cloze activity on the next page.

Book 10: Root words: 'ject', 'tract', 'port', 'struct'

Use the words from the previous page to complete these sentences.

ject = throw (from Latin)

1. When the plane caught fire, the pilot had to _____.
2. The scientists calculated the _____ of the rocket.
3. The nurse gave her an _____ion against the flu.
4. He loved her very much, but she _____ed him.

tract = pull, drag (from Latin)

1. The farmer plowed the fields with a _____,
2. A magnet _____s metal objects.
3. The dentist had to _____ the rotten tooth.
4. The student threw a paper plane and _____ed the class from the lesson.

port = carry (from Latin)

1. The policeman will _____ the road accident.
2. Many products are _____ed from China.
3. I travel to school by public _____.
4. We brought a _____ table to the picnic.

struct = pile up, build (from Latin)

1. A bridge is a _____ that carries a road across a river.
2. After the tsunami, there was total _____.
3. To _____ someone is to teach them something.
4. The essay was not clearly planned, so I had to _____ it.

Book 10: Root words 'ject', 'tract', 'port', 'struct'

GET ACTIVE IN LATIN!

ject – throw

tract – pull, drag

port – carry

struct – build

Write the words you have learned with the roots 'ject', 'tract', 'port' and 'struct' in the columns above. Choose two words from each column and write a sentence for each word.

Book 10: 4-in-a-row – 'ject', 'tract', 'port', 'struct'

construct	tractor	retract	porter	eject
inject	distract	import	report	structure
object	attract	destruction	transport	portable
instruct	export	destructive	restructure	deport
protract	reporter	projector	attractive	instruction
constructed	transported	rejected	injection	distraction

Play with two sets of colored counters. Two players take turns to read the word and put a counter on the word. The winner is the first to get four of his/her counters in a row. The winner places a counter on the trophy cup above. The game is played four times until all the trophy cups are covered. Discuss new words with the student to help develop his/her vocabulary.

Additional activities: a) Ask the student to highlight the stress in the word so that he/she can learn to pronounce it correctly. b) Ask the student to split the words up into syllables.

Book 10: Root word 'labor'

The root word **labor** comes from Latin and means 'work'.

For example: the word 'coll**abor**ate' means 'work together'.

Draw a line from the words to the correct definitions.

labored   requiring much work and effort

laboratory   worked

laborious   containing much care and detail

elaborate   to explain something in more detail than is necessary

belabor   a room or building with special scientific equipment for doing experiments

Complete the diagram below.

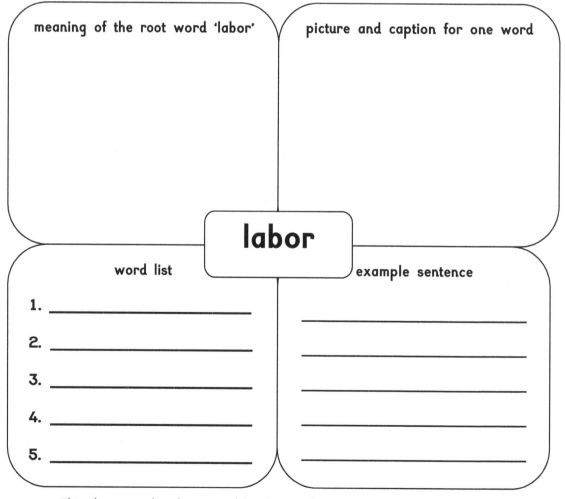

meaning of the root word 'labor'

picture and caption for one word

labor

word list

1. _____

2. _____

3. _____

4. _____

5. _____

example sentence

_____

_____

_____

_____

_____

Book 10: Root word 'fact'

The root word **'fact'** comes from Latin and means 'made' or 'done'.

For example: the word **'fact**ory' is a place where things are made.

Draw a line from the words to the correct definitions.

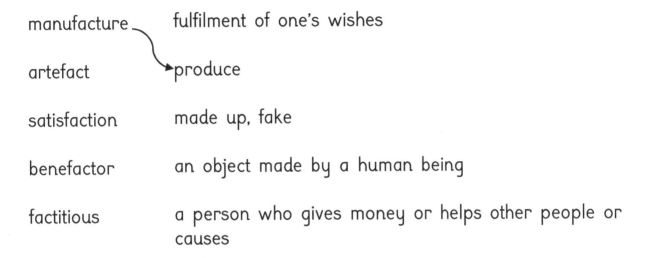

manufacture   fulfilment of one's wishes

artefact   produce

satisfaction   made up, fake

benefactor   an object made by a human being

factitious   a person who gives money or helps other people or causes

Complete the diagram below.

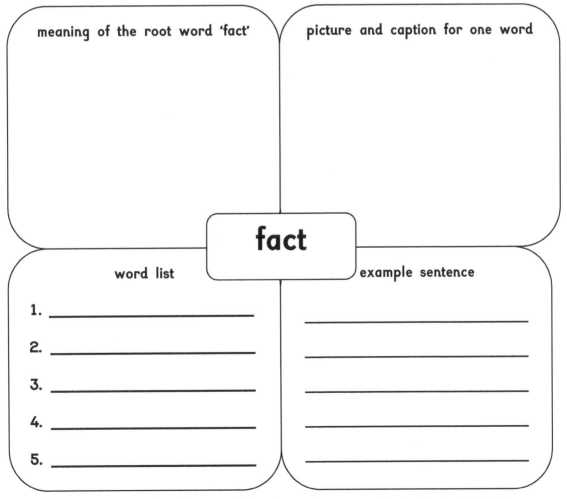

meaning of the root word 'fact'	picture and caption for one word

fact

word list	example sentence
1. _____	_____
2. _____	_____
3. _____	_____
4. _____	_____
5. _____	_____

Book 10: Root word 'form'

The root word **'form'** comes from Latin and means 'shape'.

For example: the word 're**form**' means 'make changes to something in order to improve it'.

Draw a line from the words to the correct definitions.

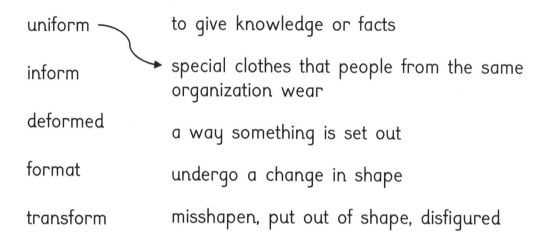

uniform   to give knowledge or facts

inform   special clothes that people from the same organization wear

deformed   a way something is set out

format   undergo a change in shape

transform   misshapen, put out of shape, disfigured

Complete the diagram below.

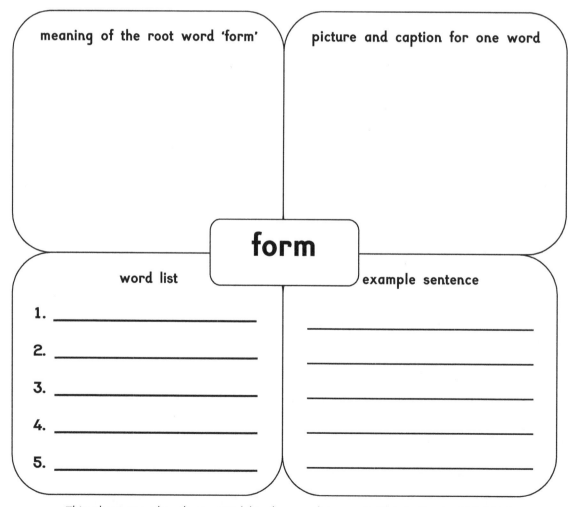

meaning of the root word 'form'

picture and caption for one word

form

word list

1. _____
2. _____
3. _____
4. _____
5. _____

example sentence

_____
_____
_____
_____
_____

Book 10: Root words 'labor', 'fact', 'form'

GET CREATIVE IN LATIN!

labor – work

laborious

collaborate

labored

laboratory

belabor

elaborate

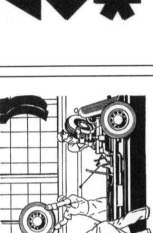

fact – made, done

factory

manufacture

artefact

satisfaction

benefactor

factitious

form – shape

reform

transform

deformed

formative

conform

uniform

Underline the root in the words above. Discuss the meaning of these words. Can you guess how they relate to the root within them? Choose two words from each column and write a sentence for each word.

This sheet may be photocopied by the purchaser. © Phonic Books Ltd 2019

Book 10: Root words: 'labor', 'fact', 'form'

Use the words from the previous page to complete these sentences.

labor = work (from Latin)

1. To _____ means to work together.
2. Scientists usually carry out experiments in a _____.
3. If you go on and on about something, you will _____ a point. You will give too much detail.
4. The necklace had a beautiful, _____ design.
5. If a job is _____, it means that it's a lot of work.

fact = made, done (from Latin)

1. _____ means artificial or fake.
2. Many people in this town work at the local _____.
3. When your wishes are fulfilled, you feel a sense of _____.
4. Many of the goods we buy are _____d in China.
5. A person who gives money to another person or a cause is called a _____.
6. The museum displayed Roman and Greek _____s.

form = shape (from Latin)

1. With one kiss from the princess, the frog _____ed into a charming prince.
2. Many people believe the tax system is unfair and needs to be _____ed.
3. To _____ is to comply with rules and laws.
4. The employee had to wear a _____ at the factory.
5. Living in another country was a _____ experience.

Book 10: Root words 'labor', 'fact', 'form'

GET CREATIVE IN LATIN!

form – shape

fact – made, done

labor – work

Write the words you have learned with the roots 'labor', 'fact' and 'form' in the columns above.
Choose two words from each column and write a sentence for each word.   © Phonics Books Ltd 2019

This sheet may be photocopied by the purchaser.

Book 10: 4-in-a-row – 'labor', 'fact', 'form'

factory	form	reform	labored	lab
laboratory	manufacture	deformed	facility	formal
artefact	collaborate	conform	elaborate	satisfaction
belabor	benefactor	formality	uniform	factitious
transform	information	formative	laborious	format
formula	formless	putrefaction	formulate	collaborated

Play with two sets of colored counters. Two players take turns to read the word and put a counter on the word. The winner is the first to get four of his/her counters in a row. The winner places a counter on the trophy cup above. The game is played four times until all the trophy cups are covered. Discuss new words with the student to help develop his/her vocabulary.

Additional activities: a) Ask the student to highlight the stress in the word so that he/she can learn to pronounce it correctly. b) Ask the student to split the words up into syllables.

Book 10: 'ject', 'tract', 'port', 'struct', 'labor', 'fact', 'form'

Insert these words into the text. Then reread the text to make sure it makes sense.

dejected – depressed, dispirited
collaborated – worked together
portable – able to be carried
satisfaction – feeling satisfied

informed – told
projected – shining out
destruction – ruin
distracted – not paying attention

The three friends spent the night in the deserted city. All around them were signs of _____: fallen columns, buildings in ruins. They were woken by a bright light shining from the orb. It _____ the shape of a tall, twisted needle onto a wall next to them.

"That clue is easy to read. It's the sorcerer's tower. I've seen it on the map," Izzy _____ them. They inspected the map closely.

Finn felt a tightness in his chest. "It's a long journey," he said wearily. He was feeling _____. They needed to find the last amber gem and release the last Guardian. They would have to face the final battle. Were they strong enough?

The three friends carried the small, _____ boat to the water and set off once more for the open sea. It was a tough journey. Time and again waves crashed over the top of the makeshift boat and drenched them. They _____ as a team, using their hands to scoop water out of the boat.

"This boat has been fantastic!" Kit patted the coracle with _____, but Finn was _____. He was anticipating the final battle of the Guardians. Would they survive it?

Book 10: Revision: prefix – root word – suffix

Underline or highlight the root words. Then write the morphemes in the correct columns. For example: re-ject-ed.

re ject ed	satisfaction	projector	portable
reporter	construction	destructive	elaborate
formal	transformed	laborious	uniform
trajectory	structure	extracted	distracting

	prefix	root word	suffix
1	re	ject	ed
2			
3			
4			
5			
6			
7			
8			
9			
10			
11			
12			
13			
14			
15			
16			

Blank morpheme diagram

Use this diagram to introduce a new morpheme to the student.

Explain the meaning of the morpheme and give an example word.

_____

_____

_____

Complete the diagram below.

meaning of the morpheme	picture and caption for one word

word list	example sentence
1. _____	_____
2. _____	_____
3. _____	_____
4. _____	_____
5. _____	_____

Blank word tree

Write the morpheme you have learned at the base of the tree. Now write the new words you have with this morpheme in the word tree.

Can you write a sentence for each of these words?

221

Word web – example page

This is a word web that can help students to revise the morphemes and words they have learned. In the center is the base or root word. The boxes on the sides list words made by adding prefixes and suffixes to the base or root word. To make your own word webs use the template on the next page.

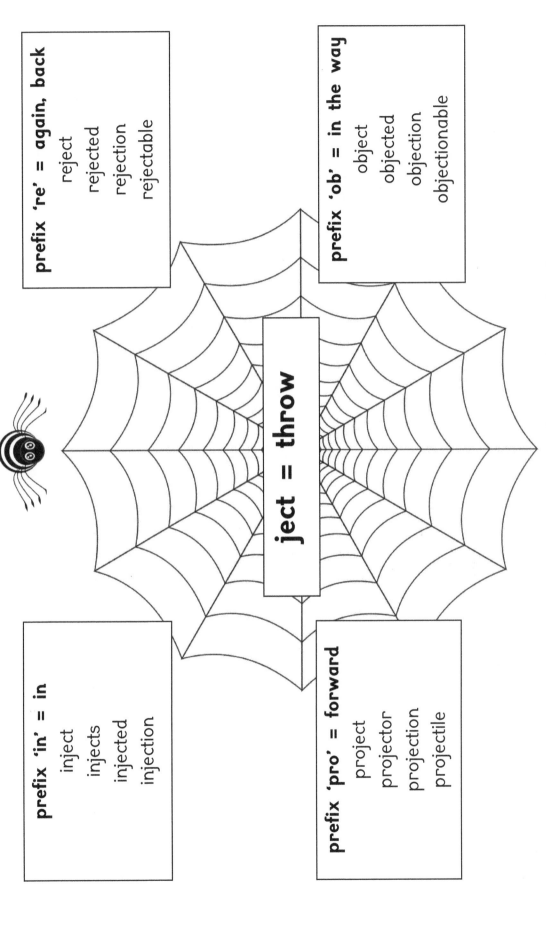

prefix 're' = again, back

reject
rejected
rejection
rejectable

prefix 'ob' = in the way

object
objected
objection
objectionable

ject = throw

prefix 'in' = in

inject
injects
injected
injection

prefix 'pro' = forward

project
projector
projection
projectile

Word web – blank page

Use this template to make a word web. Write the root or base word in the center. Add prefixes to the boxes on the sides. Make word lists in the boxes by adding prefixes and suffixes to the root or base words.

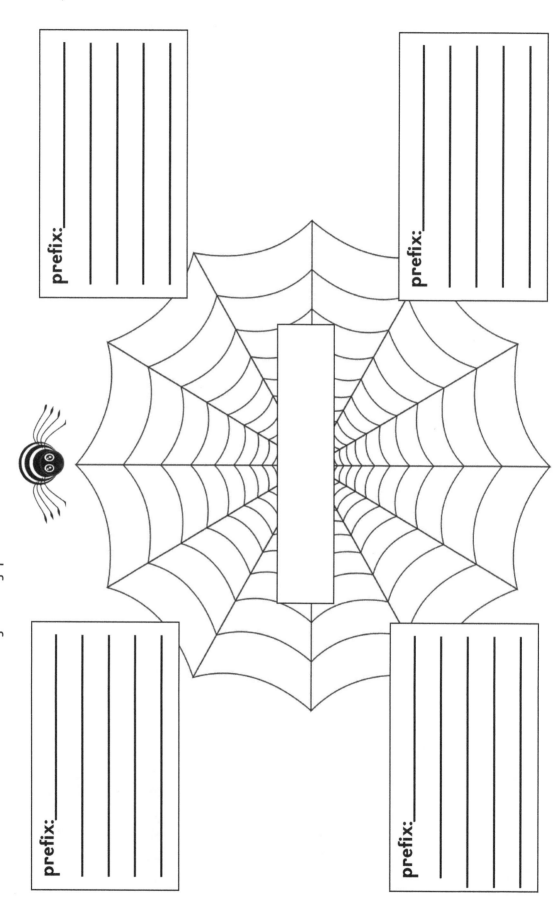

prefix: _____

prefix: _____

prefix: _____

prefix: _____

Answer sheet 1

Page 8 Activity

play, plays, playing, played, replay, replays, replaying, replayed, display, displays, displaying, displayed

Page 9 Activity

1 <u>help</u>-less 2 <u>fresh</u>-ly 3 <u>hold</u>-ing 4 <u>reach</u>-ed 5 <u>use</u>-ful 6 <u>great</u>-est 7 <u>like</u>-ly 8 <u>blind</u>-ed
9 <u>self</u>-ish 10 <u>fool</u>-ish 11 <u>speak</u>-er 12 <u>open</u>-ed 13 <u>lift</u>-ing 14 <u>end</u>-less 15 <u>hope</u>-ful
16 <u>dark</u>-en 17 <u>joy</u>-ful 18 <u>child</u>-ish 19 <u>tight</u>-en 20 <u>fight</u>-er 21 <u>neat</u>-ness 22 <u>lead</u>-er
23 <u>cook</u>-ing 24 <u>brain</u>-y

Page 10 Activity

browsing, appeared, travels, hunting, climbing, hooks, grasping, hooks, pushing, shouted, hurled, clinging, yelled, pushed, pointing, stealing, explained, pleaded, tricks, whispered, battered, notes

Page 11 Activity 1

cats, frogs, dishes, stitches, kisses, benches, wishes, batches, winters, ranches, coats, boxes, socks, watches, steps, punches, computers, buzzes

Page 11 Activity 2

boxes, batches, riches, boxes, benches, shadows, glasses, eyes, Servants, rafters, inches, smashes, crashes, directions, answers, ruins, streets, alleyways

Page 12 Activity

babies, trays, ladies, days, parties, mummies, jellies, boys, candies, valleys, cherries, joys, journeys, plays, stories, buddies, bays, puppies, days, countries, monkeys, essays, families, surveys, beauties, memories, decoys, donkeys

Page 13 Activity

/t/: looked, reached, glanced, mocked, announced
/d/: pulled, battered, damaged, gazed, rubbed, stared
/id/: dented, snorted, handed, lifted

Page 14 Activity

tapped, wagged, mended, lifted, helped, tripped, reached, plucked, moaned, peeled, dragged, printed

Page 15 Activity

ripped ripping, huffed huffing, plotted plotting, helped helping, mended mending, dripped dripping, groaned groaning, pressed pressing, bragged bragging, slammed slamming

Pages 16 and 17 Activity

scanned, followed, clutched, looked, flitted, gasped, twisted, pressed, panted, squinted, filled, wanted, slipped, sprinted, hopped, stopped, screwed

Page 18 Activity

jogged jogging, peeled peeling, begged begging, tipped tipping, helped helping, planned planning, chopped chopping, blinked blinking, picked picking, flapped flapping, jumped jumping, wagged wagging, played playing, skipped skipping, shopped shopping, mended mending, rapped rapping

Answer sheet 2

Page 19 Activity
dived diving, reached reaching, phoned phoning, hated hating, walked walking, used using, lived living, raced racing, hoped hoping, hiked hiking, bounced bouncing, liked liking, danced dancing, framed framing, trained training, arranged arranging

Page 20 Activity
waving waved, cracking cracked, blaming blamed, bragging bragged, dropping dropped, voting voted, hoping hoped, hopping hopped, mending mended, chasing chased, tapping tapped, taping taped, deleting deleted, punching punched

Page 21 Activity
using, used, useful, useless, user; hoping, hoped, hopeful, hopeless; liking, liked, likely; shaming, shamed, shameful, shameless; amusing, amused, amusement; caring, cared, careful, careless, carer

Page 22 Activity
lowered, arrived, explored, stopped, opened, grabbed, gazed, pulsed, spotted, wasted, clambered, appeared

Page 23 Activity
clambered, careful, inched, using, useless, opened, frightening, appeared, glared, hateful, faceless, being, hooded, lunged, attacked, breaking, rained, crumbled, collapsed, tumbled, raced, helpless, exploded, retreated, handed, whispered, blundered, swinging, gasping, staggered, lunged, hooded

Page 24 Activity
worried, copied, studied, stayed, denied, hurried, employed, envied, married, relied, betrayed, fancied, delayed, tidied

Page 25 Activity
copied copying, married marrying, studied studying, played playing, hurried hurrying, tried trying, carried carrying, enjoyed enjoying, buried burying, bullied bullying, cried crying, lobbied lobbying, dried drying, sway swaying, emptied emptying, replied replying, worried worrying, rallied rallying, decayed decaying, obeyed obeying, prayed praying, relied relying, delayed delaying, defied defying

Page 26 Activity
regretted regretting, profited profiting, limited limiting, admitted admitting, rebelled rebelling, omitted omitting, committed committing, exited exiting, acquitted acquitting, visited visiting, targeted targeting, permitted permitting, equipped equipping

Page 27 Activity
1 books 2 foxes 3 opened 4 reached 5 hoped 6 hopped 7 taking 8 lapping 9 carrying
10 ladies 11 toys 12 crying 13 opening 14 handled 15 tried 16 ashes 17 entered 18 babies
19 fined 20 facing 21 sitting 22 tapped 23 taped 24 denying 25 saving 26 hobbies 27 hurried
28 drying 29 having 30 stopped

Page 28
1 lamps 2 brushes 3 suffered 4 freed 5 hiked 6 plotted 7 saving 8 flapping 9 drying
10 poppies 11 activities 12 frying 13 pleasing 14 stumbled 15 pried 16 punches 17 fostered
18 cherries 19 tuned 20 chasing 21 dropping 22 dotted 23 doted 24 multiplied 25 placing
26 nappies 27 pitied 28 supplying 29 coping 30 dragged

Answer sheet 3

Page 30 Activity
Possible answers: waiter, candidate, tool, holiday, plan, chemical, action, celebration, child, granny, kite, exam, monster, sky, dictator, face, teenager kitchen, avenue, man, choir, attempt, journey, shirt

Page 31 Activity
The playful puppy chased the stick. The motherless orphan had no family. The forgetful granny lost her glasses. The moonless night was so dark we got lost. The graceful dancer took her final bow. The headless ghost visited the haunted house. The harmful chemical poisoned the water. Limitless energy means endless energy.

Page 32 Activity
fearless, wonderful, powerful, hateful, limitless, priceless, powerless, helpless, successful, careless, hopeless, tireless, wonderful, grateful

Page 33 Activity 1
forgiveness, kindness, greenness, tiredness, wickedness, sickness, deafness, neatness, brightness, fitness

Page 33 Activity 2
1 Tiredness 2 kindness 3 wickedness 4 brightness 5 fitness 6 forgiveness 7 greenness
8 sickness 9 neatness 10 deafness

Page 34 Activity 1
carelessness, cheerfulness, selflessness, wilfulness, forgetfulness, thoughtlessness, homelessness

Page 34 Activity 2
1 homelessness 2 forgetfulness 3 wilfulness 4 selflessness 5 thoughtlessness 6 carelessness
7 cheerfulness

Page 35 Activity
beautiful, spineless, clumsiness, restful, blameless, nastiness, plentiful, wordless, pitiless, hardness, forceful, bodiless, loneliness, timeless, happiness, dutiful, emptiness, mouthful, sightless, holiness, shyness, aimless, brimful, thoughtless, laziness, sleepiness, wishful, bossiness

Page 36 Activity 1
harder hardest, colder coldest, older oldest, cheaper cheapest, higher highest, greener greenest, faster fastest,

Page 36 Activity 2
1 oldest older 2 faster fastest 3 colder coldest 4 cheapest cheaper 5 greener greenest 6 harder hardest 7 highest higher

Page 37 Activity
bigger biggest, funnier funniest, finer finest, heavier heaviest, larger largest, kinder kindest, cheaper cheapest, happier happiest, hotter hottest, thinner thinnest, safer safest, sadder saddest, sillier silliest

Page 38 Activity
biggest, higher, narrowest, tallest, trickier, riskier, luckiest, longer, scarier, scariest, hotter, stronger, safer

Answer sheet 4

Page 39 Activity
Possible answers: hungrily, swiftly, deeply, soundly, carefully, slowly, gracefully, softly, quietly, closely, silently, bravely, play, shout, smile, listen, whisper, stretch, dress, battle, hold, ask, fight, demand

Page 40 Activity
lazily, hopefully, carefully, excitedly, thirstily, cheerfully, aggressively, softly, elegantly, greedily, foolishly, badly, angrily, frantically, clumsily, busily, normally, creepily, sadly, sharply, bravely, easily, narrowly, tightly

Page 41 Activity
carefully, adventurously, fearfully, safely, haphazardly, urgently, excitedly, creakily, carefully, Suddenly, cheerfully, stiffly, Finely, closely, thoughtfully

Page 42 Activity 1
weaken, gladden, widen, straighten, toughen, quicken, stiffen, flatten, loosen, worsen

Page 42 Activity 2
Lengthen, Loosen, Weaken, Harden, Darken

Page 42 Activity 3
1 widen 2 ripen 3 lighten 4 sweeten 5 quieten 6 strengthen

Page 43 Activity 1
foolish – silly, freakish – unusual, Finnish – coming from Finland, babyish – immature, ticklish – sensitive to being tickled, sluggish – slow-moving, selfish – self-centred, stylish – elegant

Page 43 Activity 2
1 selfish 2 freakish 3 sluggish 4 ticklish 5 stylish 6 Finnish 7 babyish 8 foolish

Page 44 Activity
baggy, airy, bony, skinny, foggy, cheesy, spicy, leafy, funny, noisy, icy
tasty, jumpy, runny, cuddly, curly, bouncy, choppy, giggly, shiny, itchy, leaky

Page 45 Activity
scary, darkish, spooky, quicken, hazy, bluish, tighten, creepy, whitish, freaky/freakish, smallish, bony, brutish, sharpened

Page 46 Activity 1
acceptable – able to be tolerated, breakable – capable of being broken, adaptable – able to adjust, preferable – more suitable, better, affordable – cheap enough to buy, payable – to be paid, due, transferable – able to be transferred, fashionable – stylish

Page 46 Activity 2
1 affordable 2 acceptable 3 breakable 4 fashionable 5 adaptable 6 payable 7 transferable
8 preferable

Answer sheet 5

Page 47 Activity 1

noticeable – can be noticed, deniable – can be denied, believable – can be believed, changeable – can be changed, traceable – can be traced, knowledgeable – well informed, justifiable – can be justified, desirable – wished for, movable – can be moved

Page 47 Activity 2

deceivable, compliable, serviceable, retrievable, pronounceable, removable, excusable, multipliable, valuable, unbelievable, advisable

Page 48 Activity 1

horrible – likely to cause horror, possible – able to be done or achieved, audible – able to be heard, visible – able to be seen, flexible – able to bend, accessible – able to be reached, edible – fit to be eaten, sensible – having or showing good sense

Page 48 Activity 2

1 accessible 2 visible 3 audible 4 flexible 5 possible 6 sensible 7 horrible 8 edible

Page 49 Activity 1

readable – can be read, affordable – inexpensive, possible – can be done or achieved, breakable – can be broken, fashionable – fits the latest fashion, agreeable – pleasant, audible – can be heard, approachable – can be approached, edible – fit to be eaten

Page 49 Activity 2

terrible, remarkable, bearable, speakable, horrible, reasonable, predictable, adaptable, incredible, suitable, acceptable, visible

Page 50 Activity

This shirt is reversible. You can wear it inside out too. You can't play football here. It is not permissible. I like John a lot. He is very agreeable. It is regrettable that the school trip was cancelled. The summer was very hot. In the shade it was just bearable. Number 7 is a prime number. It is divisible only by itself and 1. That ring belonged to my grandma. It is valuable. The puppy jumped up and down. He was very excitable. I believe almost anything I am told. I am very gullible.

Page 52 Activity

1 help-less-ly 2 fresh-ness 3 afford-able 4 use-ful-ness 5 care-ful-ly 6 own-er-ship 7 cream-y
8 rest-ed 9 fool-ish-ness 10 joy-less-ness 11 lead-er-ship 12 self-ish-ly 13 cheap-est
14 harm-ful-ly 15 mean-ing-less 16 fright-en-ing

Page 53 Activity

1 games 2 hutches 3 tried 4 begged 5 grated 6 rallied 7 racing 8 nagging 9 bullying 10 bodies
11 ploys 12 frying 13 useful 14 endless 15 penniless 16 happiness 17 beautiful 18 creepiness
19 bigger 20 heavier 21 hottest 22 weakest 23 carefully 24 noisily 25 normally 26 shrunken
27 shaven 28 girlish 29 regrettable 30 possible

Page 56 Activity

un-limit-ed, re-fresh-ing, hold-ing, re-place, re-use, un-like-ly, re-mind-ed, un-self-ish, im-poss-ible, dis-cover-ed, ex-port-ed, in-access-ible, hope-ful

Answer sheet 6

Page 57 Activity
Possible answers: face, behavior, visit, experience, accident, person, dog, cash, man, effort

Page 58 Activity
It will rain on Sunday so it is unlikely the festival will go ahead. A seal was spotted in the river. This is a very unusual sight. The museum visit was disappointing. It was uninteresting. Her boots were too tight. She untied the laces. As the author had died, the book remained unpublished. The digger dug up an old Roman villa. It uncovered a mosaic floor. The magician unzipped the bag and a white rabbit hopped out. Despite all the threats and bullying, the boy was unafraid to speak out. I wrote and complained many times, but the manager was unresponsive.

Page 60 Activity
incomplete – not full or finished, inaccurate – not exact, inactive – lazy or unenergetic, independent – free from outside control, inflexible – unbending

Page 61 Activity
The band played too loudly. The singer was inaudible. The party was on the beach. We were told to dress informally. She apologized, but I knew she didn't mean it. She was insincere. If you don't turn the music down, you will be inconsiderate. When I finish school, I will leave home and live independently. The old man was very weak. He was infirm. After falling off, I got straight back on the horse, but I felt insecure. The universe and galaxies may be infinite. Injustice is when people are treated unfairly.

Page 63 Activity
immature – childish, impatient – not accepting delay, imperfect – faulty or incomplete, impolite – rude, immortal – living forever

Page 65 Activity
impatient – short-tempered, impossible – can't be done, incorrect – wrong, incredible – unbelievable, insecure – unsafe, imperfect – flawed, immobile – unable to move, insincere – fake, invisible – hidden from sight, immortal – living forever, impure – mixed up with other materials, insane – mentally ill, invalid – not legally acceptable, impolite – rude

Page 66 Activity
illegal – forbidden by law, illogical – not logical, illiterate – unable to read or write, illegible – not clear enough to be read, illiberal – not tolerant

Page 68 Activity
irresistible – too attractive to be resisted, irreplaceable – impossible to replace, irrational – not logical or reasonable, irresponsible – not responsible, irrelevant – not connected to anything

Page 71 Activity
immortal – lives forever, incomplete – not whole, impossible – can't be done, inflexible – unbending, irreligious – secular, inconsiderate – not thoughtful, illogical – not rational, immobile – not moving, irresponsible – not responsible, invisible – can't be seen, impolite – rude, impure – mixed up with other materials, irreversible – can't be changed back, illegible – can't be read, impartial – unbiased, inactive – lazy

Answer sheet 7

Page 72 Activity
unfolded, impatient, unable, invisible, irresponsible, insecure, impossible, unafraid, unexpected, irrational, illogical, immeasurably, Unfrightened, incredible

Page 73 Activity
mistake – error, misspell – spell wrongly, misbehave – behave badly, mislead – deceive, misplace – put something in the wrong place

Page 74 Activity
He tried to jump over the pond, but misjudged the distance and fell in. I miscounted the number of guests. There weren't enough cupcakes. Grandad mislaid his glasses, but they were on his head. Humans should be kind to animals. They should not mistreat them. The children laughed when the teacher mispronounced my name. The criminal told lies to the police. He was trying to mislead them. The boy had the misfortune of losing both his parents. The man lost all his money. He mismanaged his inheritance. The parcel was misdirected. It was sent to the wrong address.

Page 76 Activity
disagree – have a different opinion, disconnect – detach, disobey – fail to obey, dislike – hate, dishonest – behaving in an untrustworthy way

Page 77 Activity
When I fell off my horse, I dislocated my shoulder. The man disliked crowds, so he avoided going to crowded places. It is important not to disrespect other people. The patient caught an infection, so the hospital was disinfected. The runner cheated and was disqualified from the race. If you disobey the school rules, you will be punished. The magician made the rabbit appear and then disappear. The package was damaged, so the customer was dissatisfied. The sailor disregarded the warning about the storm and he capsized.

Page 80 Activity
dislodged, disorientated, disbelief, disheartened, discover, misadventure

Page 81 Activity
1 ir-resist-ible 2 in-correct-ly 3 un-afford-able 4 mis-behav-ing 5 dis-honest-ly 6 mis-spell-ed
7 im-poss-ible 8 in-vis-ible 9 dis-obey-ed 10 il-legal-ly 11 ir-revers-ible 12 im-patient-ly
13 il-leg-ible 14 mis-print-ed 15 dis-appear-ed   16 un-self-ish

Page 82 Activity
1 unhappy 2 immortal 3 irregular 4 illegal 5 disconnect 6 incorrect 7 imperfect 8 inflexible
9 misbehave 10 discover/uncover 11 unable/disable 12 unfair 13 invisible 14 mistreat 15 misspell
16 disappear 17 impossible 18 disagree 19 incomplete 20 misdirect/indirect 21 misplace/displace
22 dishonest 23 unhelpful 24 unbutton 25 irrelevant 26 illegible 27 insecure 28 incredible
29 disobey 30 impolite

Page 84 Activity
review – a criticism of a book, film or play, revise – reread material in preparation for an exam, repay – pay back, recycle – use again, refresh – make fresh again

Answer sheet 8

Page 85 Activity

The old man could not remember where he lived. The detective had to re-examine the evidence. The kids loved to watch that video. They replayed it again and again. The food was cold when I got home, so I had to reheat it. The ball landed in the nettles. I got stung when I retrieved it. This year I didn't win the race. Next year I'll redouble my efforts. When I stood up to the bully, he didn't know how to react. Our school uniform is old-fashioned and needs to be redesigned. The tennis match resumed after it stopped raining.

Page 86 Activity

recalled, reminded, regained, repeated, rebounded, revive, responded

Page 88 Activity

preview – an advance showing of a film or play, to take precautions – take steps to prevent something bad happening, prejudice – a bad opinion formed before having knowledge of something, predict – tell the future, prophesy, premature – too early

Page 89 Activity

I predicted that my soccer team would win the match 2:1. The preview took place in a small cinema. A prefix is the part of the word that comes before the base word. There was a lot to prepare before the trip. The wedding service preceded the disco party. I pre-ordered the video before it was available in the shops. In preindustrial times, most people lived in the countryside. The firemen put out the fire quickly and prevented a disaster. We took precautions as we knew a storm was coming.

Page 91 Activity

retreated, restore, premonition, predicted, revealed, pre-packed, precaution, prevent, reacted, resumed

Page 92 Activity

postmeridian (p.m.) – afternoon, posthumous – happening after a person's death, postscript (P.S.) – an additional remark at the end of a letter, postmortem – an examination of a dead body to find out the cause of death, postpone – to arrange for something to take place at a later date

Page 93 Activity

I postponed the meeting because it snowed heavily. Postmeridian (p.m.) means 'afternoon' in Latin. Some soldiers suffer from post-war stress disorder. A postscript (P.S.) is a remark that is added to the end of a letter. A postgraduate course is for a student who has a first degree. The detective hoped to get more clues from the postmortem. A postnatal clinic is for mothers after they have given birth. Postproduction takes place after shooting a film. Some artists are only famous posthumously, after they die.

Page 95 Activity

1 antechamber 2 antisocial 3 antecede 4 antenatal 5 antihero 6 anticlockwise

Page 99 Activity

1 re-<u>fresh</u>-ing 2 pre-<u>dict</u>-ed 3 re-<u>visit</u>-ed 4 un-<u>reli</u>-able 5 post-<u>pone</u> 6 ante-<u>chamber</u>
7 dis-<u>cover</u>-ed 8 pre-<u>judge</u> 9 anti-<u>hero</u> 10 anti-<u>clock</u>-wise 11 ante-<u>cede</u> 12 re-<u>enter</u>
13 pre-<u>view</u>-ed 14 im-<u>poss</u>-ible 15 pre-<u>vent</u>-ing 16 in-<u>escap</u>-able

Answer sheet 9

Page 100 Activity

1 prevent 2 remind 3 postmeridian 4 antemeridian 5 revise 6 antenatal 7 antiseptic 8 remember
9 recover 10 predict 11 antechamber 12 precaution 13 preview/review 14 reflect 15 recycle
16 reappear 17 prefix 18 antisocial 19 prejudice 20 antidote 21 resume/presume 22 repay/repay
23 prepare 24 reconsider 25 refresh 26 reorder/pre-order 27 precede/antecede 28 postpone
29 rearrange/pre-arrange 30 reject

Page 102 Activity

unicycle – a cycle with a single wheel, uniform – clothing worn by people who belong to the same
organization, like a school, unite – come together for a joint purpose, unique – one of its kind, unlike
anything else, unilateral – affecting only one side

Page 103 Activity

My favorite character in the fantasy story is the unicorn. Panda bears are unique animals and must be
saved from extinction. In circus school, one can learn to ride a unicycle. School uniforms make everyone
dress the same way. Many workers joined the union to fight together for their rights. The universe has
millions and millions of galaxies. I may go to a university after high school. After the disaster, the people
united and helped one another. One army made a unilateral decision to stop fighting the war.

Page 105 Activity

bilingual – speaking two languages fluently, bimonthly – occurring every two months or twice a month,
biped – an animal that uses two legs for walking, bilateral – affecting two sides, binoculars – field
glasses (with a lens for each eye)

Page 106 Activity

When I ride my bicycle, I put my helmet on. If you are bilingual, you can speak two languages fluently.
Humans walk on two feet, so they are bipeds. Birdwatchers use binoculars to see the birds close up.
The biweekly magazine arrives every two weeks. A bimonthly check-up is a check-up every two months.
Twice a year, the family has a biannual holiday. Bilateral symmetry is when two sides are exactly the
same. To bisect means to cut something into two halves.

Page 108 Activity

tricycle – a vehicle with three wheels – one at the front and two at the back, triceratops – a herb-eating
dinosaur with three horns, trio – a set of three people or things, trident – a three-pronged spear often
depicted with the god Poseidon, trilogy – a group of three related novels, films or plays

Page 109 Activity

The author is writing the third book in the trilogy. A triangle has three sides and three angles. Young
children ride tricycles because they can't balance well. If you triple the number 3, you get the number 9.
My dad is trilingual. He speaks English, French and Spanish. The Greek god Poseidon is usually shown
holding a trident. In next year's triathlon, I will be running, swimming and cycling. Triceratops were
gentle herbivores. The musical trio played the piano, flute and violin.

Page 111 Activity

quadruplets – four babies born in one birth, quadruped – an animal that has four feet, quadlingual –
having knowledge of four languages, quadrilateral – a shape with four straight sides, quadruple – to
multiply something by four

Answer sheet 10

Page 112 Activity
A square has four sides and four angles, so it is a quadrangle. The mother needed extra help to look after her quadruplets. The Olympic Games are quadrennial (occur every 4 years). If you quadruple the number 5, you get the number 20. Many people in Europe speak four languages. They are quadlingual. Horses, goats, dogs and cats are quadrupeds, but humans are bipeds. A circle divided into quarters has four quadrants. A Roman chariot drawn by four horses is called a quadriga. To quadrisect means to cut something into four parts.

Page 114 Activity
December – the tenth month of the Roman calendar, decathlon – an athletic competition in which the competitor participates in ten different events, decimate – to kill or destroy a large proportion, decimal – a system of numbers based on the number ten, decimeter – one tenth of a meter

Page 115 Activity
I am 25 years old and a decade ago I was 15. December used to be the 10th month in the Roman calendar. A decimeter is a tenth of a meter and is ten centimeters long. A decapod has five pairs of walking legs, like a crab or lobster. The hurricane decimated most of the trees in the forest.
In elementary school we learned how to use decimals and fractions. Decalogue is another word for the Ten Commandments. A decathlon competition includes ten different athletic sports. A decagon is a shape with ten sides and ten angles.

Page 117 Activity
centimeter – a measurement of one hundredth of a meter, percent – a part in every hundred,
cent – one hundredth of a dollar, centigrade – the Celsius scale of temperature,
centenary – one hundredth anniversary of an important event

Page 118 Activity
The industrial revolution began in the 18th century. In the future, many people will live to become centenarians. A dollar is one hundred cents. A dime is ten cents. Fifty percent is the same as a half of something. A centipede is an arthropod with many legs. I had to shorten the curtains by ten centimeters. The temperature was 30 degrees centigrade in the shade today. There was a centenary celebration of the author's death. A centurion was a commander in the Roman army.

Page 120 Activity
1 triangle 2 bicycle 3 century 4 quadruped 5 decade 6 unique 7 uniform 8 decimated
9 trilingual 10 quadruple 11 triplets 12 centimeters 13 unicorn 14 decathlon 15 bilateral

Page 121 Activity
multinational – including or involving a number of countries, multitude – a large number of people or things, multiracial – made up of or relating to people of many races, multiply – increase a number by multiplication, multimillionaire – a person who possesses many millions of dollars

Page 122 Activity
A multitude of people came to the demonstration. If you multiply the number 3 by 5, you get 15. The children learned to sing their multiplication tables. A rainbow is multicolored because it has seven colors. The United Nations is a multinational organization. A multisyllabic word is a word with more than one syllable. In Europe many people grow up multilingual. The multimedia exhibition included painting, sculpture and video art. At the food festival we tasted delicious multi-ethnic foods.

Answer sheet 11

Page 124 Activity
trio, multicolored, century, combined, multiple, centimeter, united

Page 126 Activity
1 multi-<u>color</u>-ed 2 un-<u>afford</u>-able 3 tri-<u>angle</u> 4 dis-<u>regard</u>-ed 5 per-<u>cent</u>-age 6 ante-<u>chamber</u> 7
re-<u>enter</u>-ed 8 pre-<u>vent</u>-ed 9 anti-<u>clock</u>-wise 10 bi-<u>cycle</u> 11 <u>dec</u>-ade 12 mis-<u>spell</u>-ed
13 in-<u>access</u>-ible 14 uni-<u>form</u>-ed 15 multi-<u>ply</u> 16 uni-<u>verse</u>

Page 127 Activity
1 uniform 2 bicycle 3 triangle 4 centiliter 5 decimal 6 unicorn 7 bilingual 8 multinational
9 multiple 10 universe 11 unilateral 12 triple 13 multiply 14 centimeter 15 centigrade
16 centipede 17 tripod 18 triplets 19 quadrant 20 triceratops 21 multitude 22 multiracial
23 university 24 union 25 unify 26 binoculars 27 bisect 28 decimate 29 biceps 30 triathlon

Page 130 Activity
submerge – cause something to be under water, subtract – take away, submissive – obedient and
passive, subterranean – existing or occurring under the earth's surface, subcontinent – part of a
larger continent that covers a land mass

Page 131 Activity
The fishing nets got tangled with the submarine's propeller. Hippos spend sixteen hours a day
submerged in rivers and lakes. The prisoners escaped through a subterranean tunnel. The newsletter
had many subscribers. I submitted my application for a job at the museum. North America is a
subcontinent of the continent of America. The police managed to subdue the angry protesters.
The dog lay on its back in a submissive posture. When I got paid, I had to subtract the money I
owed my parents.

Page 133 Activity
superior – higher in rank or quality, superficial – occurring or existing on the surface,
supersonic – involving a speed greater than sound, supernatural – relating to something that can't be
explained by the laws of nature (like a ghost), superhuman – showing exceptional abilities or powers

Page 134 Activity
I grazed my knee, but the wound was not deep. It was superficial. They needed superhuman effort to
swim to the distant shore. Superman is a superhero from a comic published in America in 1938.
My new bike is superior to my old bike because it has better gears. The teacher supervised the class
while they took their exam. The superintendent oversees other workers in the factory. Many people
believe in supernatural powers. In the US, basketball players are superstars. Supersonic aircraft
travel faster than the speed of sound.

Page 136 Activity
transfer – to move from one place to another, translate – to express words in another language,
transform – to make a change in the nature, appearance or shape of something,
transfusion – the transfer of blood from one person to another, transparent – you can see through it

Answer sheet 12

Page 137 Activity
The man lost so much blood he needed a transfusion. To transcribe something is to write something that is spoken. The first nonstop transatlantic flight took place in 1919. The windows must be transparent so people can see through them. The Harry Potter books have been translated into many languages. In the story 'Beauty and the Beast', the beast transforms into a prince. Stained-glass windows let some light in as they are translucent. The football player was transferred to a better football club. To reduce pollution people must use more public transport.

Page 139 Activity
interact – to talk or do things with other people, interrupt – to stop a person speaking by saying something, intermission – a short period between parts of a play or concert, interfere – to involve yourself in a situation when your involvement is not wanted or helpful, intercom – an electrical device that allows one-way or two-way communication

Page 140 Activity
The spy intercepted the message hidden in the picture frame. The internet has changed the way people communicate. Interrupting is rude and people should wait for their turn to speak. In the intermission, Mom bought ice cream for everyone. It is best not to interfere in matters that don't concern you. When the old lady did not answer the intercom, we began to worry. The cogs interlocked and the engine began to turn. To save the environment, we must all sign an international agreement. There was a fight and the teacher intervened to stop it.

Page 142 Activity
export – to send goods or services to another country for sale, extract – to get, to pull or draw out, exhume – to dig out something buried in the ground, especially a corpse, excursion – a short trip or an outing, exhale – breathe out

Page 143 Activity
The student was expelled from the school for bullying behavior. The dentist extracted the rotten tooth using a local anaesthetic. The USA imports more products than it exports.
The detective wanted the body exhumed from the grave. We went on an excursion to the Natural History Museum. Many people escaped from the cruel dictator and lived in exile.
An extrovert is someone who is outgoing and socially confident. Luckily, the bomb exploded in a field, away from people. To inhale means to breathe in and to exhale means to breathe out.

Page 145 Activity
exotic, submerged, exposed, exploring, transparent, interrupted, supernatural, transformed, transfixed, interwoven, extended

Page 147 Activity
1 ex-<u>port</u>-ed 2 ex-<u>pect</u>-ed 3 super-<u>human</u> 4 inter-<u>rupt</u>-ed 5 tri-<u>angle</u> 6 trans-<u>form</u>-ed
7 sub-<u>scribe</u> 8 pre-<u>view</u>-s 9 in-<u>cred</u>-ible 10 uni-<u>corn</u> 11 trans-<u>atlantic</u> 12 sub-<u>marine</u>
13 pre-<u>dict</u>-ed 14 ex-<u>pell</u>-ed 15 inter-<u>connect</u>-ed 16 super-<u>star</u>

Answer sheet 13

Page 148 Activity
1 submarine 2 transparent 3 interrupt 4 internet 5 transform 6 superficial 7 transfer
8 international 9 exclude 10 superhuman 11 expel 12 submerge 13 translate
14 transport 15 interfere 16 extract/subtract 17 explode 18 interlock 19 express
20 subscribe 21 transfusion 22 intermarry 23 expect 24 intercept/except 25 transmit
26 superior 27 subtract/extract 28 extrovert 29 exhume 30 supernatural

Page 150 Activity
magnate – a person who has great power, magnify – to make something appear larger,
magnanimous – showing great generosity, especially in forgiving injury or insult, magnifier – an
instrument like a lens that makes something appear larger, magnitude – great size

Page 151 Activity
We used a magnifying glass to investigate the wing of an insect. The magnate donated millions of
dollars to charity. People didn't realize the magnitude of the disaster. The view from the top of the
tower was magnificent. To be magnanimous is to show great generosity to others. The magnifier
made the seed look many times larger.

Page 153 Activity
megalith – a large stone in a prehistoric structure (like Stonehenge), megabyte – a large unit of
computer memory, megalomania – an unnaturally strong wish for power and control, megaphone
– a cone-shaped device that makes one's voice louder, megalosaurus – a large carnivorous
dinosaur from the mid-Jurassic period

Page 154 Activity
The megalosaurus was a large carnivorous dinosaur. This memory card holds 1 megabyte of
memory. The leader needed a megaphone to be heard above the noisy crowd. Megalomania is an
unnatural desire to have power and control others. No one knows exactly why these megaliths
are placed in a circle. 'Megalopolis' is a Greek word for a very large city. Last year, no one had
heard of the band and now they are megastars.

Page 156 Activity
minimize – reduce to the smallest possible amount, minimum – the least or smallest, minuscule –
tiny, extremely small, minor – lesser in importance, minority – a smaller number, less than half of
the whole

Page 157 Activity
As part of our minibeasts project, we studied spiders and beetles. Minigolf is a fun game for the
whole family. The doll's house has miniature furniture and miniature figures. The miniskirt became
fashionable in the 1960's. The majority of students have a T.V. at home. A minority don't. It was
only a minor accident. Luckily, no one got injured. Everyone should be able to earn a minimum
wage.

Answer sheet 14

Page 159 Activity

microchip – a small piece of silicon inside a computer, microwave – an oven that uses waves of energy to cook or heat food quickly, microscopic – so small it can only be seen using a microscope, microbe – a tiny organism, like bacteria, microcosm – a small community or place that reflects something bigger

Page 160 Activity

Mom said you mustn't put the metal dish in the microwave. A microlight is a very light, small airplane for one or two people. My dog was microchipped so he can be found if he runs away. The popstar sang into the microphone. I plan to study microbiology at university. The scientist studied the microbes under the microscope. Germs are microorganisms that cause diseases.

Page 162 Activity

minuscule, megastructure, magnificent, diminish, minimal, microscopic

Page 164 Activity

1 re-<u>mind</u>-ed 2 micro-<u>phone</u> 3 re-<u>treat</u>-ed 4 mega-<u>store</u> 5 ex-<u>tend</u>-ed 6 magni-<u>fy</u>
7 mini-<u>mum</u> 8 inter-<u>act</u> 9 im-<u>poss</u>-ible 10 mini-<u>bus</u> 11 dis-<u>appear</u>-ed 12 mega-<u>lith</u>
13 ex-<u>plain</u>-ed 14 micro-<u>wave</u> 15 inter-<u>fere</u> 16 micro-<u>organ</u>-ism

Page 165 Activity

1 megahit 2 magnify 3 minibus 4 minigolf 5 microwave 6 megabyte 7 microchip 8 microscope
9 microbiology 10 microphone/megaphone 11 minibike 12 magnificent 13 microchip 14 megastar
15 megalomania 16 magnate 17 magnanimous 18 minuscule 19 miniature 20 minimize
21 magnifier 22 megadose 23 microcomputer 24 megalosaurus 25 megalith 26 minicab
27 microlight 28 magnitude 29 microcosm 30 minimal

Page 168 Activity

captain – a person in command of a ship or team, cap – a soft hat with a peak, caption – a heading that goes with a poster, illustration or photo, decapitate – cut the head off (someone), behead, capital letter – an upper case letter used at the beginning of a sentence, for proper nouns and acronyms

Page 169 Activity

manicure – a cosmetic treatment for hands and nails, manacles – handcuffs, manufacture – to produce something on a large scale using machines, manuscript – a book or document written by hand, manage – to handle something and take control of it

Page 170 Activity

inspect – to look at something closely and critically, respect – to admire someone, suspect – to believe someone is guilty of a crime, spectator – a person who watches a show, game or event, perspective – a point of view

Page 171 Activity

pedestrian – a person who travels on foot, biped – an animal that walks on two feet, centipede – an arthropod that has many segments, each with a pair of legs, expedition – a journey or voyage to discover new places or things, pedometer – an instrument that records the number of steps taken

Answer sheet 15

Page 173 Activity
1 capital 2 cap 3 capital letter 4 decapitate
1 manicure 2 manacles 3 manage 4 manual
1 suspect 2 Spectacles 3 respect 4 spectator
1 biped 2 pedals 3 pedestrian 4 expedition

Page 176 Activity
biography – a story of someone's life written by someone else, biodegradable – something that can be broken down slowly by natural processes, biodiversity – the variety of life, autobiography – a story of someone's life written by that person, amphibian – an animal such as a frog that can live on land and in water

Page 177 Activity
survive – to continue to live in spite of danger or hardship, vivid – strong, distinct, such as a vivid memory (like real life), vivacious – lively, bubbly, like a vivacious young girl, vivarium – a tank for keeping animals in (like an aquarium for fish) vital – essential

Page 178 Activity
mortuary – a place where dead bodies are kept before burial or cremation, mortally – in a deadly or fatal way, mortified – to feel very embarrassed or ashamed, mortician – a person who prepares the dead for burial, immortal – to live forever

Page 180 Activity
1 biodegradable 2 biography 3 amphibian 4 Biodiversity 5 Biology 6 autobiography
1 vivarium 2 vivacious 3 vital 4 survived 5 vivid 6 revived
1 postmortem 2 mortified 3 mortuary 4 mortician 5 immortal 6 mortal

Page 182 Activity
amphibian, perspective, capital, decapitated, managed, vivid, biodiversity, mortally, survived

Page 184 Activity
1 res-pect-ed 2 bio-logy 3 re-vive 4 sur-viv-or 5 man-acles 6 capit-al 7 im-mort-al
8 centi-pede 9 ped-als 10 bi-ped 11 per-spect-ive 12 spect-acles 13 man-age 14 in-spect-ion
15 ped-lar 16 de-capit-ate

Page 186 Activity
predict – to say what will happen in the future, dictator – a ruler with total power over a country,
dictionary – a book that lists words and their meanings, contradict – to say the opposite,
dictation – the act of speaking words that are written down by someone else

Page 187 Activity
A dictator is a ruler who has total control and power of a country. The teacher gives the class a spelling dictation every Friday. The actor didn't speak clearly, so she had to improve her diction. To contradict someone is to say the opposite of what they said. 'Bene' means 'good', so the word 'benediction' means 'a blessing'. Nowadays, students prefer to use an online dictionary. An edict is an announcement or command made by a king. The weather man predicted rain on the weekend.

Answer sheet 16

Page 189 Activity
autograph – a signature, especially one written by a celebrity for a fan, paragraph – a unit of writing, usually a few sentences about one central idea, photograph – a picture made using a camera, graph – a chart or diagram, bibliography – a list of books that are mentioned in a book

Page 190 Activity
Geography is the study of the Earth's surface, climate and peoples. Cartography is the study of the drawing of maps. A paragraph is a unit of text centered on one idea. A graph is a diagram that shows information in a visual way. An autograph is a signature usually written by someone famous. A biography is a written account of a person's life. A photograph is a picture made by a camera. After she retired, the Prime Minister wrote an autobiography.

Page 192 Activity
scribble – to write something in a careless or hurried way, subscribe – to sign up for something and receive it on a regular basis, prescription – an instruction written by a doctor ordering treatment for the patient, manuscript – a book or document of music written by hand, postscript – P.S. – an additional remark added to the end of a letter

Page 194 Activity
remember – to bring to one's mind, recall, recollect, memo – a short written message from one part of an organization to another, memoir – a biography or historical account written from personal knowledge, memorial – a monument built to remind people of a person or an event, memorabilia – objects that are collected to remind one of people or events

Page 195 Activity
The boss sent out a memo to let everyone know about the meeting. My first memory goes back to age two, when I was stung by a bee. Every year we commemorate the soldiers who died in the wars. When the Prime Minister retires, she will write her memoirs. My father collects memorabilia of his favorite football team. My class traveled to France to visit a war memorial for World War I. Stonehenge has been standing there from time immemorial.

Page 197 Activity
predicted, described, topography, contradict, remembered, memories

Page 199 Activity
1 pre-dict-ted 2 contra-dict-ed 3 geo-graph-y 4 auto-graph 5 manu-script 6 pre-script-ion 7 dict-ate 8 re-mem-ber 9 mem-oir 10 bio-graph-y 11 script-ure 12 sub-scribe 13 e-dict 14 in-scribe 15 para-graph 16 de-scrib-ing

Page 202 Activity
eject – to throw something out in a violent or sudden way, inject – to introduce a liquid (like a vaccine) into the body with a syringe, interject – to interrupt, project (verb) – to stick out, trajectory – the path of a missile traveling through the air

Answer sheet 17

Page 203 Activity
tractor – a powerful vehicle with large wheels, used for pulling farming machinery, distract – to pull attention away from something, retract – to pull back from something, attract – to draw towards something, traction – have a grip or ability to drag

Page 204 Activity
porter – a person employed to carry luggage at a station or hotel, deport – to send someone away from a country, export – to send goods to another country for sale, transport – to carry people or goods from one place to another by car, train or plane, support – to give assistance

Page 205 Activity
structure – something built, like a building, bridge or dam, restructure – to organize differently, construction – the action of building, destruction – the act of destroying, instruct – to tell someone to do something or to teach a subject or skill

Page 207 Activity
1 eject 2 trajectory 3 inject 4 reject
1 tractor 2 attract 3 extract 4 distract
1 report 2 import 3 transport 4 portable
1 structure 2 destruction 3 instruct 4 restructure

Page 210 Activity
labored – worked, laboratory – a room or building with special scientific equipment for doing experiments, laborious – requiring much work and effort, elaborate – containing much care and detail, belabor – to explain something in more detail than necessary

Page 211 Activity
manufacture – produce, artefact – an object made by a human being, satisfaction – fulfilment of one's wishes, benefactor – a person who gives money or helps other people or causes, factitious – made up, fake

Page 212 Activity
uniform – special clothes that people from the same organization wear, inform – to give knowledge or facts, deformed – misshapen, put out of shape, disfigured, format – a way something is set out, transform – undergo a change in shape

Page 214 Activity
1 collaborate 2 laboratory 3 belabor 4 elaborate 5 laborious
1 Factitious 2 factory 3 satisfaction 4 manufactured 5 benefactor 6 artefacts
1 transformed 2 reformed 3 conform 4 uniform 5 formative

Page 217 Activity
destruction, projected, informed, dejected, portable, collaborated, satisfaction, distracted

Page 218 Activity
1 re-ject-ed 2 satis-fact-ion 3 pro-ject-or 4 port-able 5 re-port-er 6 con-struct-ion
7 de-struct-ive 8 e-labor-ate 9 form-al 10 trans-form-ed 11 labor-ious 12 uni-form
13 tra-ject-ory 14 struct-ure 15 ex-tract-ed 16 dis-tract-ing